SPORT

Also by Mick Cochrane

Flesh Wounds

SPORT

MICK COCHRANE

University of Minnesota Press
Minneapolis / London

Copyright 2001 by Mick Cochrane

Originally published by Thomas Dunne Books, an imprint of St. Martin's Press, 2001.

First University of Minnesota Press edition 2003

Published by the University of Minnesota Press
111 Third Avenue South, Suite 290
Minneapolis, MN 55401-2520
http://www.upress.umn.edu

A Cataloging-in-Publication record for this book is available from the Library of Congress.

Printed in the United States of America on acid-free paper

The University of Minnesota is an equal-opportunity educator and employer.

12 11 10 09   10 9 8 7 6 5 4 3

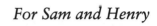

For Sam and Henry

Acknowledgments

For support while writing this book, I am grateful to Canisius College, in particular, to President Rev. Vincent M. Cooke, S.J.; Vice President for Academic Affairs Herbert J. Nelson; and Dean of Arts and Sciences James P. McDermott.

Lon Otto read several drafts; it's not possible for me to say how much I appreciate his criticism and his friendship. Thanks, too, to a number of other friends who read the manuscript: Duff Brenna, Jack Williams, Lance Wilcox, Ron and Marlys Ousky, Paul Schmidt, Paul Von Drasek, Ricki Muller, and Nancy Jones. Jim Hanneman and Nancy Ann Hanneman provided useful information.

I am profoundly grateful, finally, to Melissa Jacobs and Jay Mandel for the passionate attention and critical intelligence they've brought to my work, and to my wife, Mary, as always, for her patience, assistance, and faith.

SPORT

CHAPTER ONE

On the red baseball jersey I wore the summer between seventh and eighth grade, it said WEST SAINT PAUL across the front, and on the back, in the same cheap white iron-on lettering, it read GUS LUND across the shoulders, with a big number 13 in the middle, and on the bottom, OIL. It was a big shirt and I was a skinny kid, so the bottom of OIL tended to get tucked in. At a time when major league ballplayers were beginning to wear their names on their backs, it would be natural to think that the player wearing that jersey was named Gus Lund. Gus was a good baseball name, I'd always thought—much better than my real name, Harlan, which always sounded to me like the name of a professional bowler or an obscure vice president—and when it became a kind of nickname for me among my teammates, I didn't mind. "Come on you Gus," my buddies would holler from the bench when I'd step up to the plate. "Show 'em where you live." Actually, our team was sponsored by the Smith-Dodd Businessmen's Association, and each businessman got himself one of our players to use as a kind of human billboard: Lou Chimera was Dodway Barbers, Marty Hauser was Ed's Mel-O-Glaze Bakery, Eddie Doyle was Jim's Meats, and I was Gus Lund Oil.

Gus Lund was the man who came to our house every six weeks or so during the winter—in Minnesota, that's November through April—and brought fuel for our ancient and hugely inefficient furnace. He'd pull up in his truck and fill the tank, standing there patiently in the cold, stamping his feet and exhaling big cloudy bursts of smoky breath, just like a guy pumping his own at a Mobil station. When he was done, he stuck the bill in the door and drove off. I don't remember anything else about him. He was just a grown-up guy who performed a function, like the doctor or the mailman. He wore a fur cap with earflaps. I remember the tremendous furrow the hose made in the snow as he dragged it from his truck in the alley to the back of the house, like the tread of a prehistoric snake.

My life away from baseball, meanwhile, had grown unspeakably strange, like a dream you remember as you tell it over breakfast but break off because it's just too far-fetched, too embarrassing. Two years before, when I was in fifth grade, my mother, bedeviled by inexplicable falls and blurred vision and numbness in her hands and feet and phantom burning sensations, underwent a battery of tests—I can remember being afraid of the sound of the phrase "spinal tap"—and had been diagnosed with multiple sclerosis. She announced this to my older brother Gerard and me during the first and only family meeting we ever held. Sitting at our Formica kitchen table with a cup of coffee and a smoldering Pall Mall, she pronounced the name of her condition with a kind of reverent dread, a mixture of horror and pride.

"Things are going to change around here," she said.

When she dropped things now, it wasn't funny anymore. Every spill meant something, and if she tripped, her fall foreshadowed some unspoken, inevitable misery. Our neighbor's Aunt Madge had MS, too. We used to watch as Mr. Whelan carefully unloaded her from the car when she'd arrive for holiday visits, settled her in a wheelchair, bundled and propped her with shawls and blankets, and bumped her awkwardly up the porch steps. She was blind and drank through a straw with desperate breathy gasps as someone held her glass. Bedsores were a problem, and going to the bathroom was complicated and unpleasant.

What my father was like before my mother got sick, I can hardly remember. He was a trial lawyer, a hard drinker, inclined at home to quiz us over dinner about current events and to argue with my mother using elaborate accusatory gesticulations—courtroom flourishes, presumably—that my brother imitated flawlessly behind his back. "Is it not true?" Gerard would ask, pointing his pudgy finger at me like a conductor's baton, brandishing it like a switchblade, waving and wagging it in the air, finishing always with an emphatic corkscrew.

What I remember best are the accessories of my father's job: the long yellow pads, a battered leather briefcase with a broken clasp, a drawer full of laundered white shirts, which we would plunder for the cardboard. And I remember particular acts of violence marked by scars in our house like commemorative plaques: the time he smashed a plate of spaghetti against the kitchen wall or gouged the plaster with the telephone or kicked out the bathroom door or nicked a cupboard with a highball glass.

My mother's disease did not make my father heroic or nice or even sane. He stayed downtown later and later, drank more, shouted more. He began to direct his violence at human targets. On Thanksgiving the year before, my brother and I were in the kitchen playing a board game, Stratego, while my parents argued in the living room. The Lions game was on the television, and my father, who'd slept most of the day, was getting louder and louder. Gerard and I listened and stared silently at the red and blue pieces, the mustached spies, the colonels with their extravagant plumed hats, the hidden bombs. We heard a crack, a fleshy explosion, and then a gasp and a dull thud. When we scrambled into the room, we saw him standing over my mother and our springer spaniel Heston, his head lowered, circling him, growling and snarling. My mother was flat on her back, bleeding from the nose and mouth.

"Leave me alone," she said, and my father turned and walked away. I put the dog outside and Gerard got some ice.

Early the next morning, my father packed a suitcase and disappeared quietly into a taxi cab. I heard the front door slam and looked down from my bedroom window as he put his bag in the trunk and eased into the backseat. Gerard, still half-asleep in the bottom bunk, a big blanketed mass, asked me what was going on. I understood in my gut exactly what was happening, but I didn't know what to call it. I didn't know the words.

"Nothing," I said. "Shut up."

Papers were filed, child support ordered, visitation negotiated, and a divorce decreed. But after one month— one tense visit to the zoo, one check—it all stopped, as if having fulfilled his obligation once, my father saw no need to repeat it. And so, despite my mother's sporadic efforts to secure legal redress—she'd spend a morning on the telephone, mostly on hold, and eventually dissolve into tears of frustration—we descended abruptly into a kind of poverty that in our middle-class neighborhood seemed to be a social blunder, an affront to propriety, like a loud stereo or a junked car or a ragged lawn, an act of bad taste, not something anyone would talk about or be so rude as to notice. My mother cashed the AFDC check across town, and having bought one bundle of food coupons, couldn't bring herself to use them.

Things got disconnected, turned off. Like the telephone. So we hoarded dimes and jogged up to the booth at the corner and left that space on the school forms blank, like you forgot to fill it in. One day a fellow jumped off an orange city truck and planted a spade in our front lawn and had his hand on the water valve before my mother headed him off at the curb with a handful of singles she pilfered from my brother's newspaper collection shoe box. When they came for the car, I was sitting on the front steps listening to a Twins game on a transistor radio. The repo man, a fat guy in plaid slacks, waved to me from the street and asked me what the score was, and then he got in our family Ford and drove it away. Just like that.

A sympathetic neighbor gave my mother a work-at-home project: assembling his company's manuals for vending machine repair. For weeks we lived among stacks and stacks of photocopied diagrams and schematics, exploded views and numbered bolts and tables of specs, spread across the dining room table, on the chairs, the piano bench, on top of the refrigerator. We all worked at it spasmodically, but there was a page missing, and another got misplaced, and it was boring, and things toppled and got spilled, and finally we dumped it all in big cardboard boxes and stashed them down the basement.

Gerard brought home two gallons of yellow paint and a roller from Coast-to-Coast one afternoon and took a few swipes in the living room and then lost interest. Weeds grew in the front yard. We ate food out of boxes and cans, standing up. My mother bought a three-pronged metal cane at a garage sale and slept a lot. Heston ran away and got hit by a car; we found him one morning at the curb, wrapped in a bloody bedspread. Something terrible was happening and I had no idea what to do about it.

Meanwhile I went off to school, and like my brother, a bright enough kid, made A's on my schoolwork. I solved word problems with one and two variables, memorized vocabulary words and used them dutifully in sentences, constructed a beautifully layered model of the earth's atmosphere with glue and clay and food colorıng, like a fancy parfait. I was a polite and well-behaved twelve-year-old, the kind of student teachers say is a pleasure to have in class. But after school, in the afternoon, I would walk home very, very slowly. I'd stop at Muller's Drugs and read comic books, watch them unload vegetables at Applebaum's, pet the Griffins' collie through their Hurricane fence. Home at last, I'd take a deep breath on the porch and one last look around before stepping through the front door, like somebody about to dive underwater.

Once I tried to organize the wicker basket my mother devoted to our family's finances. I must have believed that if I could only bring some order there, it would begin to set things right somehow. It was a rat's nest of papers, mostly old bills, gas and electricity and telephone and water and insurance and JCPenney and Sears and Standard Oil, many of them still in coffee-stained envelopes, unopened. There were canceled checks and bank statements and overdraft notices and collection letters, one less understanding and more demanding than the last; exotically colored food stamps like foreign currency; and a paper-clipped bundle of grocery store coupons neatly clipped from the Sunday supplement for Shredded Wheat and toaster waffles and orange juice, all of them expired. And there were at least half a dozen invoices from Gus Lund, each one written in the awkward scrawl of a man wearing gloves, recording the date and number of gallons pumped, and in the amount due box, a short horizontal line.

I should say now that I appreciated this, this coincidence, or irony, or whatever it was, that this small businessman who put my beloved baseball shirt on my back was the same man who kept my house warm and, with that little horizontal line, showed me a glimpse of forgiveness and generosity in that bucketful of adult complexity and indifferent insistence.

I should, but it's not true. This is the truth: I gave up and piled everything back in that basket and tried my best to forget about it, tried to believe that all would be well. And then in May, I tried on the jersey our coach, Mr. Walker, tossed at me after practice, wrinkled and smelling of mothballs, and I wore it with unthinking delight every Tuesday and Thursday that summer on the ball diamond, where miraculous comebacks were always possible, where I still knew the rules.

CHAPTER TWO

George Walker taught history and driver's education at the senior high school, and even though it was hard for me to imagine him in a classroom, pulling down maps, wearing a chalky blazer, lecturing about the Whiskey Rebellion and the Missouri Compromise, he must have been an ideal driving instructor—infinitely calm, unflappable, chatty, not a guy to ride the chicken brake.

Unlike some other coaches in our league who wore their teams' uniforms the way big league managers do, Mr. Walker just wore Bermuda shorts and polo shirts and a dusty canvas golf hat, the kind that comes in a tube. He never argued with the umpires or rode the opposition or yelled at his players. During games he kept the book and coached third base with a flair we attempted but could never duplicate. He kept up a constant stream of hopeful, encouraging nonsense, musical and automatic as a carnival barker's, like a man speaking in tongues, variations improvised on our names, on the situation, even the weather, like an ancient singer of tales. This was big-league chatter. And the signals themselves, real and phony, indicators and wipe-offs and red herrings, so expressive you might have thought he was signing the game for the hearing impaired. He'd touch skin to skin, go to the letters, the belt buckle, the top of the cap; he'd lay his finger aside of his nose like Santa Claus and point to various parts of his anatomy as if you'd never seen an elbow or an earlobe before.

Mr. Walker was an old ballplayer himself, a pitcher who made it all the way to Triple A ball, the story went. Though soft around the middle, when he threw BP, you could see in him what fans still pay to see at old-timers games: the outlines of grace, slowed down, softened by middle-aged paunch, but never completely obscured. He could throw strikes forever, break off one identical slow curve after another, and when he was feeling playful, mix in an eye-popping knuckleball, which he later taught me to throw (it's the fingertips, he explained, not the knuckles, and it will wiggle only if you throw it hard, don't push it).

At practice he was a kind of traveling baseball tutor, hanging onto the batting cage one minute and telling you to keep your weight back, on the mound the next, holding runners with the pitchers. He showed me footwork at first base so intricate that I had to practice at home with a sofa pillow for the bag until I could shift my feet without thinking. He'd stand on the mound and point with a fungo bat as he taught us complicated cut-offs and bunt defenses and pick-off plays and then whoop with pleasure when we executed a maneuver properly.

Best of all was the end of infield practice, once the

infielders had scooped up bunts and fired the ball home and left the field one by one, when Mr. Walker would hit our catcher a towering foul pop-up. It's not easy to hit a ball straight up in the air—try it some time—but he never failed to connect, one higher than the last, and Willie Myers would wobble underneath it and wait and wait, and, finally, gather it into his big floppy mitt and return to the bench grinning. When the other team's coach would complete their drill by *throwing* a ball into the air for his catcher, we'd exchange glances on the bench, then look away in embarrassment, knowing right then and there that we'd kick their sorry butts.

Most of my teammates knew Mr. Walker only on the field, but I lived down the street from him and his wife—they had no children—and when I helped Gerard with his route, delivered their newspaper. I used to supply my buddies details concerning his home life which we found fascinating. During the summer they grew fabulous roses in the backyard and sat side-by-side in lawn chairs on the deck, George wearing his hat, of course, sipping iced tea and reading the newspaper and listening to big band music on a portable radio. One night, I saw them on the deck dancing.

"No shit?" the guys said. "Dancing? Come on."

"Really," I said. "The jitterbug or something."

Lately, Mrs. Walker had been sick, and he'd been going to the hospital three and four times a day.

We were a well-coached team with lots of good players—three went on to play ball in college, and one, Willie Myers, signed a professional contract—and we won lots of ballgames, and though not at all a talented

athlete, I never embarrassed myself. I had good soft
hands at first base and saved our shortstop plenty of
errors by scooping his short-hop throws. I knew the
strike zone and took my share of walks, and because I
was willing to let the ball hit me, I hung in against
curveballs and popped my share of dinky singles over
the second baseman's head. And I became a terrific
bunter. Even today, if you put me in the box and
instructed me to lay one down, I could do it: Square
around, keep the bat level, and give with the ball—
pretend you're going to impale the ball with a big nail,
Mr. Walker told us. First or third base line, you tell me.

I never hit a home run, but I did win a game with a
bunt. In the bottom of the seventh in a tie game against
Burnsville, with Marty Hauser on third, Mr. Walker
signaled for the suicide squeeze—pointing to his wedding band, the indicator, then the sign, left hand to the
right elbow, acknowledged by my tossing a handful of
dirt—and though it was a terrible pitch, high and outside, I got my bat on it, Marty thundered across the
plate, and I was a hero for a night, all because Mr.
Walker knew what I could and couldn't do. When he
took us to Dairy Queen afterward, he made much of
buying me an extra-large cone, with sprinkles, a kind of
edible award I would have had bronzed if I could.

And then one Tuesday in June he didn't show up for
the Cottage Grove game. We sat on the bench and put
on our cleats and blew bubbles and chewed sunflower
seeds and sized up the opposition and waited for Mr.
Walker and his duffel bags full of bats and balls.
Finally, we had to improvise. The umpire had some

bases in the trunk of his car, and we borrowed a game
ball and a batting helmet from the opposition. Willie
Myers hit infield and made the lineup and no one
beefed. Everybody used Eddie Doyle's own gigantic
Adirondack bat, his personal model which normally he
jealously guarded on the bench, hefting it between
innings and rubbing it endlessly with a tarry rag, Lord
knows why. The little guys choked up, and the on-deck
man, without a bat to swing, touched his toes and
stretched, as self-conscious about his arms as a new-
comer on stage. That bat had gotten four straight hits in
the third inning and knocked across three runs when
Mr. Walker's station wagon pulled into the parking lot.
The fellow driving, a spitting image of Mr. Walker, only
younger and thinner, no hat—it had to be his brother—
dragged the equipment bags over to our bench and told
us that George was sorry, he couldn't make it tonight,
Mrs. Walker had passed away.

A group of us agreed to attend the wake together. I
found a clean shirt in my closet, and with some impatient instruction from my mother, I got one of my
father's old ties decently knotted. She knew how, but
her hands were too awkward to do it herself—that's
what made her mad, I could tell. To my mother, her disease was not a tragedy, not the bogeyman Crippler of
Young Adults described in the public service television
commercials—it was an insult, a form of insubordina-
tion, her body's nose-thumbing refusal to carry out simple commands.

"You sure you want to go?" she asked. She knew I'd
never been to a funeral before. When our dog got

killed, it was my mother who'd taken care of it. I wanted no part of it.

"Sure," I said.

At the funeral home Mr. Walker looked dazed, not so much grief-stricken as profoundly uncomfortable. This wasn't something you could practice for, and nobody is very good at it. There was nothing to chatter about. He was wearing a gray suit and a red tie. His thinning hair was slicked back—I'd never seen him before without a hat—and there was a cut on his chin, stopped with a sliver of white tissue. We watched him sweating and smiling and shaking hands with a stream of little elderly women in black hats. He nodded in our direction, and we stood in line quietly and signed the guest book, one after another, handing the black ballpoint chained to the desk on to the next fellow as if it were Eddie Doyle's bat.

It was a closed casket, thank goodness, which I knelt in front of momentarily, as if in prayer. The casket itself struck me, who knew nothing of such things, as extraordinarily heavy and ornate, plated and armored somehow, not the plain wooden box I had expected. On top was a photograph of Ann Walker: A surprisingly young woman with tight black curls and brown eyes, buttoned into a mackinaw and framed by brilliant red and orange foliage, she was smiling broadly, not stiffly posed like a studio shot, but with her whole face, as if whoever held the camera had just cracked a joke and she was on the verge of a full-blown, joyously undignified belly laugh. Next to the photograph was a glass vase holding a single white rose.

We hustled outside into the late afternoon sunlight and the sounds of traffic on Robert Street, where Mr. Walker joined us on the front steps. He loosened his tie and asked about the Cottage Grove game. He told us that batting practice was at five o'clock on Tuesday, same as usual. He shook hands with each of us, his big pitcher's hand enveloping ours, and thanked us for coming. "I appreciate it," he told us. "More than I can say."

When my turn came, I wanted to say something, about his wife maybe, tell him that I really was sorry and felt sad. And there was still more I wanted say, things I knew but couldn't put into words, not then, not now, but I was nervous and nothing came out.

CHAPTER THREE

I can remember staring through my brother's pudgy fingers at the furious glare of a single laminated eyeball, no bigger than a pea. "Well?" Danny Sellers said to me, and took a drag from the one of the Old Golds he had lifted from his father. "Well?"

I was in a neighbor's garage, being quizzed on my baseball card collection. "He's st-st-st-stumped," Brett Krueger said. He stammered and always smelled faintly of his mildewed basement bedroom, but it was his garage, a big double complete with a built-in workbench, full of drawers and compartments, which housed Brett's extensive collection of skin magazines. Gerard had been bragging to his friends that I could identify any player from the smallest exposed part, and now I was being put to the test.

"Dick Radatz," I said. "The Monster."

"I can't fucking believe it," Danny Sellers said.

He fished another card from my box, and covered up all but an ear, which I recognized immediately as belonging to Milt Pappas. It wasn't hard. It's not as if I had practiced or possessed a photographic memory or anything like that. I just knew. I really *knew* these guys, the way you know your friends or your parents. I spent more time with them—studying, sorting, arranging—than I did with any three-dimensional human being. Who couldn't recognize his best buddy's nose or his dad's chin? I did a few more. The bill of Gino Cimolli's cap, Juan Marichal's foot, a freckle on the nose of Ron Fairly, Wally Bunker's left nostril.

"Good," Gerard said. That I was a kind of idiot savant reflected well on him, and I could tell that he was pleased. "Now get lost," he said, and I took my box of cards and beat it.

My brother was a fat boy. There was one in your grade school class. He wore street clothes in gym class and couldn't do a single pull-up. At lunch you would catch him looking longingly at your cupcakes. He never asked, but if you offered, he always said yes. All his school pictures show deep-set eyes and a big piggish grin, a boy trying way too hard, no idea how to approximate real kid joy. He had wide flat feet—13 EEE, in tenth grade, I seem to recall—which I always associated with his being overweight. As a result, he could wear only plain-toe black dress shoes, like a mailman. He was only fifteen years old, but in his crewcut and bland Jerry Leonard Big and Tall Man clothes—button-down shirts, golf sweaters—he gave the impression of being a small-scale, prematurely middle-aged man, somebody's sitcom dad.

To me, Gerard's size was not so much a condition developed over time—obesity—as a given, something essential about him. He was always big, for as long as I could remember. That's who he was. Still, sometimes I wondered. How come Gerard was fat and I wasn't? How come he was always hungry? Sometimes I'd watch him eat, working his way mechanically, joylessly through a bag of chips or a box of cookies, and it seemed to me that he was possessed by something, in the grips of something urgent and insatiable. I knew I could never ask him what it felt like; I knew there were no words for that. So I was left to wonder and worry.

Only years later did I get an inkling of how hard it must have been to be him. In a bag of old clothes headed for Goodwill, I found a pair of Big Mack jeans, the kind favored by the guys with beer guts and jack-hammers, waist sizes running into the fifties, legs like elephants', the only jeans that fit my brother. On the back pocket of this pair, in black magic marker, was a crooked lightning bolt, his own pathetic do-it-yourself designer jeans.

He was habitually self-conscious, always guarded, trained by years of ridicule to be wary of new opportunities for exposure and humiliation. He never took his shirt off in a public pool, never rode a bike. Just the winter before, he had gone ice skating for the first time. We started going to the Dodway rink, my brother and I, behind what used to be a library, on Saturday and Sunday mornings. He'd found a big fancy pair of hockey skates somewhere and wanted to try. We'd go early, early in the morning, at five, five-thirty, when it was still dark. That way, we had the rink to ourselves and I could shoot a puck around, which wasn't normally allowed. And there was no audience, nobody there to laugh.

The warming house was locked, so we'd sit in the snow and lace up our skates. It was so quiet we could hear the traffic signal at the corner click with every change of the light. At first, my brother just stood on the ice, getting the feel of the skates, a wobbly, woolly giant. I put my shoulder to him, padded in his parka, and pushed him like a stalled car across the rink. Then he took some short experimental strides on his own. Slowly he got the hang of it, and before long, he was gliding across the ice on his own, grinning. He never fell. We'd circle each other in the dark for a half hour or so, work up a sweat, the early morning silence broken only by the sound of skate blades scraping against the ice and our own heavy breathing. On those few mornings, we enjoyed a kind of dreamy, unobserved, wordless camaraderie we felt nowhere else. When it started to get light, and the fog lifted, and the city buses started to rumble by, we'd put on our boots and head home.

We shared a bedroom grudgingly, like longtime warring rivals reconciled by the most tenuous truce. On my side, I piled my clothes and schoolwork and sports magazines and the TV-sized cardboard box that held my baseball cards. At night, Gerard would lie in his bunk reading, and I would commune with those cards. I'd pore over them, the image on the front, the statistics on the back, reading the narrative arc—variously triumphant, tragic, or comic—encoded in each career record. I invented an indescribably complex game that allowed me to oppose two teams with a coin and a die.

I was in deep, way deeper than any kid I knew. My friends at school bought cards, some traded them, but many of them had given it up, lost interest, gone on to something else. None of them had my all-consuming passion. They didn't need them the way I did. As much as I loved the game of baseball—following the Twins day by day on the radio, playing ball myself—I think I loved my baseball cards even more. For me, they weren't so much things to possess as a place to be, a safe and vivid universe to inhabit, the same way readers live in their beloved books.

That summer I was obsessed with Tony Oliva, the Twins' right fielder, his baseball card, which for some reason seemed impossible to get. Pack by pack, I put together nearly a full set of cards, superstars and common players, team cards and league leader cards, and the checklists, which I despised. I visited different stores, like a desperate gambler looking for a lucky slot machine, and pulled one pack from the bottom of the box, one from the top. I accumulated innumerable stiff sticks of powdery pink gum. I got doubles, triples, something like seven or eight Bill Monbouquettes. But still no Tony Oliva.

I needed that card, don't ask me why. Maybe because as a ballplayer, Tony O was everything I was not. Back then, before the knee injuries and surgeries that would eventually cripple him, he was a fleet-footed, strong-armed outfielder. He was a slashing, bad-ball hitter. He had quick, powerful wrists, what Mr. Walker called a

fast bat. He didn't need spring training or batting prac
tice; he hit line drives in March—he was a natural.

Several years before, in his rookie season, he had visited my grade school. He spoke no English and an
injured knuckle prevented him from signing auto-
graphs, but there in the school library, dressed in a
checked sport coat and white shirt and what was almost
certainly a clip-on tie, accompanied by big Jim Lemon,
the Twins' first base coach, he exuded a playful, devilish
charm. He smiled and waved and put a stick of chewing
gum into his mouth. And while Coach Lemon described
what Tony meant to the ball club, he flicked the balled-
up gum wrapper over a throng of fourth graders at red-
haired Miss Meegan, the music teacher. When she
looked sternly in his direction, he smiled back, all innocent bewilderment.

He knew the language, I suspected then, and a lot
more besides. His real name was Pedro Oliva, but he
had escaped from Cuba using his brother's papers. It
was a good story, and the Twins' broadcasters loved to
repeat it. But I couldn't help but wonder sometimes
about the real Tony Oliva, Pedro the ballplayer's
brother, still stuck in Cuba. He could read his own
name in the box scores, maybe hear it on the Spanish
language broadcasts. What about him? He'd been left
behind, his name stolen, his identity usurped. Nobody
talked about *him*. Nobody—except me, apparently—
seemed to feel even a little bit sorry for him. Nobody
else seemed to brood about him.

Anyway, Tony Oliva was my favorite player, and I
wanted his card. I wanted it because I didn't have it. It

was that simple. And the longer I didn't have it, the more cards I collected that were not Tony Oliva, the more I wanted it. I felt desire like a physical sensation, a burning in the throat.

Most of the time, Gerard professed disdain of me and my obsession. He wasn't interested in baseball. His hobbies were aeronautic, martial. On his side of the room were model airplanes—Spitfires, Lightnings, Japanese Zeros, Mustangs, and Flying Tigers complete with grinning jagged teeth. There were stacks of magazines devoted to World War II weaponry. He did warships, too, the *Bismarck*, a whole fleet of cruisers and destroyers, carefully glued 16-inch gun turrets on the USS *Nebraska*. At a garage sale, he picked up a pile of Avlon Hill board games, and from time to time we'd spread the thousand little pieces on the floor—blue for the Allies always, the bad guys a suspicious pale pink— and attempt to fight the Battle of the Bulge. There was a cupful of dice and long tables of combat factors. We didn't have a rule book, so we made up a lot. My brother would come at me with his Panzer divisions, and when things started to look bad for me, I'd quit, which drove him nuts. But the Americans were supposed to win. It made no sense. Why did the Nazis have all the high numbers?

At night, in our bunks, we'd sometimes talk a little, but not much. We never mentioned our father, though I thought about him and suppose Gerard did too. We didn't really discuss the way things were falling apart at home, either. The water heater broke one day, and it didn't get replaced. For baths we heated water on the kitchen stove in saucepans and ran it up the stairs to the tub. We just did it; we didn't talk about it.

Mostly, we'd argue, sometimes halfheartedly, sometimes heatedly, depending on how things stood between us, about his radio, which I wanted turned down, and about the closet light, which I wanted to leave on. He always won. The implicit threat of physical force—he'd pound me if I didn't give in—always succeeded in the end. Most of the times he did actually hit me, oddly enough, were when I was asleep. I would sometimes grind my teeth at night, or so Gerard told me, and when I did, he would get out of bed and give me a good hard slap in the face.

I admired my brother, and I worried about him. He was smart; he understood things. He could explain why a curve ball curved, tell you the name of the combustible gas in farts. He knew something about what was going on with our mother, some kind of neurological scarring, why she was only going to get worse. The fall before, he had become a student manager for the B-squad football team, the guy who carries the bag of balls and tapes ankles. It was a marginal kind of belonging: he couldn't wear a uniform, but he got to ride the team bus. As a result, he had a reason to hang, however peripherally, with some of the cool guys, Danny Sellers included, his neighborhood pal, a speedy wide receiver destined now for big things on the varsity. Gerard brought home ice packs and pungent plastic jars of Atomic Balm from the locker room along with some new obscene locutions, which I cautiously tried out on my junior high friends.

He got good grades in school. Still, I heard things.

"Your brother puked on our front steps last night," Stevie Krueger, Brett's brother, told me one day at Harmon field.

"What?" I said. "What?"

Grinch is what most kids called Stevie. He had the same long face and pinched, malevolent features as the cartoon villain. "It was disgusting," he said. "We had to hose down the steps. The welcome mat still reeks."

"He was sick?" I said.

"Sick?" the Grinch said. "Right. You could say that. He was smashed. Paralyzed. I've never seen anybody so wasted."

Gerard had started smoking, too, not just an occasional weed, but the real habit, his own brand even, Marlboros. I found full packs stashed in his dresser drawers. He took to gobbling Lifesavers at home, but wintergreen or not, I could still smell smoke. It clung to him, his hair, his clothes, even his belongings, his school papers and magazines, so that after a while, our bedroom, whether he was in it or not, smelled like cigarettes. Finally he started to light up right in our room. He'd prop himself with pillows and a book and smoke one after another. I never said anything and neither did he. It was business as usual. But with a butt dangling from his lip, he looked like a different person.

I'm not sure why this all bothered me so much. It's not that I had moral objections. I'd done plenty of bad things myself and aspired to do worse given half a chance. Maybe it just seemed unworthy of him, the slosh and stink of it, the midnight puke. Probably I just didn't want him to grow up, to do what they did. I understood that one day he would; I just never imagined that it might happen so fast. I didn't want to lose him, not yet, not so soon. I was afraid he was going to leave me completely alone, up to my neck in it still, with no one in the other bunk, nobody even to battle with.

I decided that I needed to do something. But what? I couldn't imagine having a heart-to-heart with my brother. We weren't Wally and Beaver by a long shot. If I did manage to say something to him—what? what would I say?—I knew he would laugh at me, or worse. He could wither me with a single contemptuous look, bust me with one punch. Finally, I decided to do it in writing. I scribbled a handful of notes—DON'T DRINK, was all I could think to write, DON'T SMOKE—and folded one into his sock drawer, tucked one into his shirt pocket, slipped another into his math book.

For the next few days, I just watched him. I tried to read his expression when he came downstairs in the morning, studied him while he ate his Frosted Flakes. The more I watched him, the more suspicious, potentially duplicitous, even guilty he seemed. This is the nature of surveillance, I suppose, the ordinary magnified and sifted and scrutinized. But it was nothing particular, no sign anyway that he had read my messages.

Then I found one of my notes in the bottom of the bathroom wastebasket. The piece of paper was not even crumpled. Gerard had just dropped my note in the trash, casually and dispassionately discarded it, it seemed to me, like a piece of junk mail.

That same day I got Tony Oliva. I was riding my bike aimlessly on the west side after supper, and just as it was starting to get dark, I stopped at a place on George Street that my mother always called the junk store. It said JJ'S on a sign out front, but JJ was long gone. An older woman ran the store these days. Gray and round-shouldered, wrapped as always in a dark sweater, she was standing behind the counter smoking, staring off in the direction of the beer cooler. She looked startled when I came in, not necessarily pleased.

The store sold dented canned goods, stale beef jerky, crappy toys on spinning racks. There were boxes of open cartons in the aisles spilling forth a bounty of odd-ities: ketchup and mayonnaise in containers big as paint cans, outdated cardboard desk calendars adorned with the smiling faces of All-State agents, custom-printed paper napkins commemorating other people's special occasions: GOD BLESS YOU MABEL MOORE, HAPPY ANNIVER-SARY JERRY AND WANDA, GOOD LUCK FRED! In the back of the store, there was a fish tank and a real piranha, which, if you flicked the glass, would show its teeth. There was a mangy green-eyed cat curled up on a win-dowsill. The junk store was a spooky museum, full of musty surprises. It scared me, and I loved it.

The baseball cards were on a lower shelf, jammed together with boxes of dusty, unwrapped penny candy. I grabbed two packs, put my money on the counter, and stepped outside to sit on the curb and open them in private. To this day, although I have never played the lottery, not once scratched off an instant winner, never picked six or laid down a dollar in hopes of becoming Set for Life, I think I understand the appeal, the feeling of anticipation and possibility, same as tearing into a pack of new cards. Like Christmas—this time, it might really be a puppy—only you can do it again and again, as many times as you want, at least until you run out of money.

I found Tony O at the bottom of the second pack. He was kneeling with his Louisville Slugger, resplendent in his home whites, blue sky and palm trees in the background, wearing the same sly smile he had showed Miss Meegan.

I placed the card carefully in my shirt pocket and rode home, rapturous, practically dizzy with fulfillment. Gerard wasn't home, so I showed it to my mother, who made a sound signaling acknowledgment if not interest, and I lay in bed a long while studying it, front and back, Tony's vital statistics, hits and runs, RBI and stolen bases, his enigmatic smile, and finally fell asleep thinking about them, Pedro and Tony, the batting champion and his distant brother.

A few days later I made one more attempt to reach my brother. I wrote some more notes, same messages, plus a new one, an abject one-word poem. PLEASE, I printed on the last piece of paper, and slipped it in his wallet.

My brother never responded directly this time, either. But the next day I found something in my own dresser drawer. It was Tony Oliva, torn precisely into four neat pieces.

I tried to tape the card back together. Can you imagine? It was never any good after that.

CHAPTER FOUR

My father was not out of the picture, not yet. He came back from time to time, at odd hours, always more or less in the bag. He'd stand on the front steps—my mother would never let him in—and shout through the screen door. Lord knows what he wanted. To get some last licks in on my mother, I guess. Still looking for the last word.

"Bitch," he would snarl. "Gimp."

My mother rose to the occasion. The MS had done nothing to slow her tongue. She'd lean on her cane in the doorway and give it right back to him—as well or better than she received. My brother and I stayed back, but we could smell him, the stale stink of smoke and booze.

"Sot," she called him, my mother's invective always slightly archaic, as if drawn from dusty books. "Whoremonger."

I remember thinking at the time that the name had a certain ring to it, even pronounced "hoor," as my mother did, a kind of dated dignity. Eventually my mother would get tired, need to sit down. She would slam the door dramatically and lock it with a flourish. But he never wanted to go away.

One time he moved around the side into the back-yard—Gerard and I followed him, charted his course, window to window—nosed around in the garage, brought out a handful of tools, and finally fell asleep in the metal-frame hammock. We watched him out there, swaying slowing back and forth, the outlines of his body impressed on the canvas. When it started to get dark, my mother gave me a dime and ordered me to the corner booth to call the police.

"My dad's causing trouble," I said, something like that. A patrol car showed up twenty minutes later with a couple of beefy, well-scrubbed suburban cops, sheepish and polite. They conferred with my mother and went around back.

"Mr. Hawkins?" one of them said. We were watching through the window. "Mr. Hawkins?" By this time he was snoring, loud. The cop gave his shoulder a soft, almost affectionate shake. My father brushed him off and turned over. The cops shrugged. What are you gonna do?

One of them explained it to my mother. He was only sleeping, after all. He hadn't broken any law. "But if there should be a problem," he said, "give us a call. By all means." He tipped his cap.

"Stupid sons of bitches," she said as they ambled to their car.

She put a radio in the back window and cranked it up

full blast. She turned on the backyard floodlight and flicked it on and off.

"Souse," she hollered out the window. "Sleep it off somewhere else."

Finally my father got up, stiff and slow, rubbing his neck. He picked out something from the pile of tools at his feet, and headed out, cursing and waving a red pipe wrench in the general direction of our house, like some half-crazed, vengeful mechanic.

Another time, after a brief, almost perfunctory, couple of rounds with my mother, he planted himself on the curb in front of our house. It was a mild evening in July, the smell of barbecued chicken was in the air. Gerard was out with his pals. I'd just gotten home from a ball game and still had on my jersey and stirrup socks. My father sat there, hunched in his blue suit, his chin resting on his hand. He looked simultaneously sad and sinister somehow, scowling at the kids circling in the street on their bikes, a glowering suburban gargoyle.

As it got later and later, it became apparent that he wasn't going anywhere. It was like a sit-in. He would not be moved. "What's he doing?" my mother wanted to know.

"Nothing," I said. "He's just sitting there."

"I'll be damned," she said.

She clattered around the living room with her cane, humming while she pondered her next move. She respected my father, if only as an adversary still capable of surprise, who could still rouse her to exertion, bring forth her best effort. She scooped up a pile of bills from the wicker basket on the mantel, where I had stashed it after unsuccessfully straightening it out earlier.

"Here," she said, and shoved a handful of envelopes into my hands. "Take these out and give them to him. Tell him you're tired of eating macaroni."

"Mom," I said.

"Do it," she said.

So I did. Moved cautiously down the walk and stood beside him for a moment before I spoke. "Hi, Dad," I said.

He looked up. "Hey, Sport," he said.

He was wearing sunglasses, and there was something about them—they were too small, the lenses dark circles the size of silver dollars, crookedly set on his nose—and the tilt of his head suggestive somehow of blindness. I could imagine grotesquely rolling eyes, irises clouded with milky cataracts. I sat down beside him.

"Whatcha got?" he said.

I handed him the bundle of bills. "From Mom," I said.

"No problem," he said, and slipped it smoothly into the inside breast pocket of his suit coat, that dark, mysterious, silk-lined region, the male marsupial pouch.

"So what's new?" he said. "How's tricks?"

"We won tonight," I said. "I got two hits."

One was feeble, true, a weak grounder that died in the long infield grass, but they all look like line drives in the box score. That's what Mr. Walker liked to say.

"Good," my father said. "Good for you."

We sat there together on the step, neither of us saying anything more after that, just staring into the street. I liked sitting there with him, side by side, not talking. It was like fishing, what I imagined fishing was like. We were waiting for the bus that never comes. The world seemed more interesting somehow, more vivid. Across the street, Mrs. Gunsher, who was old and nosy and kept the baseballs that went into her yard, who kept an eye on neighbors' comings and goings with a pair of field glasses, was crouched in her flower garden, trowel in hand, frozen, like a rabbit, practically quivering with watchfulness. The sun was setting orange, and I could hear what sounded like fireworks in the distance, and, for the moment, I could almost believe there was no problem. My father pulled a bent cigarette from a crumpled pack of Camels and lit up. He held the pack out to me. "No thanks," I said. He was kidding, I'm almost certain.

My mother was watching me from the house, I knew, unhappily, no doubt, wondering what in the hell I was doing, but I didn't look back. We sat there for a good while, maybe fifteen minutes, maybe a half an hour, maybe even longer, I can't say for sure. It started to get dark, and Mrs. Gunsher finally went inside. We could see her television flickering through her front window.

And then suddenly, just as my father's breathing got regular and a little loud, and I was almost certain he had nodded off, a big black car roared around the corner and pulled up in front us at the curb, facing the wrong way. A man got out. The engine was running, the lights on, radio playing. He was wearing baggy plaid shorts and rubber sandals.

"Hawk," he said. "You scoundrel."

I knew him. His name was Charlie O'Connell. He was a lawyer, too, a friend of my father's from law school who had, according to my father anyway, flunked the bar exam so many times he had a favorite seat, next to the window.

"Charlie," my father said. "I'll be a son of a bitch."

Years ago, when my parents were still entertaining, when Gerard and I used to dine on cocktail wieners before being bathed and confined to the upstairs in our pajamas and left to peer through the banister at the party below—the smoke and laughter, the merry tinkling of ice, my mother in a dress—Charlie O'Connell was among the regulars. Since then, he'd become a figure in local politics, a gadfly, the St. Paul paper called him, the watchdog of City Hall.

He put his arm around my father and winked at me. He led him to his car and deposited him in the front seat. I never discovered how he came to show up just at that moment. Maybe my mother contrived it somehow. I wouldn't put it past her. Maybe it was part of his watchdog duties, maybe just an accident. It didn't seem that strange to me. Things happened, first one thing and then something else. I was never surprised, and I never asked why.

I watched the red taillights of Charlie O'Connell's car disappear and headed back inside. I was afraid that my mother would give me hell, but she had, it turned out, sunk again into her usual torpor. She was sitting at the kitchen table, her legs resting on an empty beer case, staring blankly into the Thursday newspaper grocery ads—grapes, lettuce, pineapples, everything on sale.

After that, with Charlie O'Connell's help, I believe, my mother got a restraining order. She received a piece of paper in the mail, the order signed by a judge, which she read and reread with something like joy. If she had asked me, I would have told her how likely I thought my father was to be restrained, just how inclined he was to follow orders.

Two weeks later, having fallen asleep listening to a Twins broadcast from the coast, I was awakened in the middle of the night by the sound of breaking glass and my mother's cries. My father had returned once again, no longer pacific and contemplative, in no mood to chat. Once again, my mother, who had taken to sleeping on the living room couch because she had such a hard time climbing stairs, refused to let him in. She must have had some words for him. So he found a baseball bat in the garage—my 31-inch Little League Louisville Slugger—and took it to the side door. He had always hated doors, being shut out; when he used to bust up our house from the inside, that's what he went for, doors, to our bedrooms, the attic, even closets, punched and kicked out their plywood center panels like a martial arts expert with a single sharp—and presumably satisfying—jab.

I found Gerard downstairs standing in the hallway in his underwear, frozen, crying and screaming, snot streaming from his nostrils, pointing to the door. The window had been smashed, but jagged shards of glass still stood in the frame. My father was on the back stoop, hissing threats, beating a murderous, insistent rhythm on the door. In the yellow glow of the back door lamp, framed in the broken window, his face was a fiendish rubber mask, purpled and contorted with rage and exertion.

He reached through the broken window, groping blindly, his arm like a sinewy, twisting, angry snake. My mother was kneeling on the floor, glass in her hair, her hand covering the lock, a red claw. She was sobbing.

"Please, Hawk, please. Stop," she said. "Stop now."

He found her hand and started to beat it with his fist, his forearm like a short, powerful hammer. But it was my mother's right hand, the side of her body numbed by disease, so dead to any feeling she could burn herself and sense it only through the smell of her own flesh. There was the sound of a sickening human splintering, bone and cartilage, but she never let go.

"I'll kill you," he said, "I'll kill you all," and I believed him. There was blood spattered on the door in elaborate arcs and complex glistening whorls, like the squirt-and-spin paintings I made at the state fair, broken glass glittering maliciously on the floor. My brother was making a squeaking sound, his chest heaving with convulsive sobs, and there was a sound coming from me, too, I think, no words, just hysterical hiccups, my own midnight scat song of pure terror.

When I saw the door start to give—the wood split-

ting, the hinges starting to heave and buckle, I swear—
that's when I did it. I ran. Turned on my mother and
brother and left them, an act of pure, unalloyed cow-
ardice, flung open the front door and sprinted out of the
house, down the steps and into the night. I ran down the
sidewalk past the darkened houses of our neighbors,
through the circles of light cast by the street lamps overhead, my mother's cries and my father's curses growing
fainter and fainter the farther I ran.

CHAPTER FIVE

George Walker answered the door wearing pajamas, matching tops and bottoms, navy blue with red piping, so neat they looked pressed, or fresh from the package maybe, the pins just removed. That image—a middle-aged man in flannel nightclothes—triggered in me some deep, inarticulate longing, for things that matched, for domestic order and stability. I used to study them in the Gokey's Christmas catalog, these people in pajamas, slippered in soft leather and robed in Tartan plaid, purebred retrievers curled at their feet on sweet-smelling, cedar-filled beds. That's what I wanted, I never told my mother, not the nightshirts and long johns, nothing lined with fur or filled with goose-down, not even a compass or utility knife. I wanted those lives, that world, where you hung up your clothes and brushed your teeth, where one day resembled the next, no explosions of broken glass in the middle of the night, no bad checks, nothing incurable. He was a widower himself, of course, I couldn't forget that, but even his grief, I imagined, was contained and ordered somehow. It meant something, I believed. It made some kind of sense.

Mr. Walker squinted down at me through his black-framed bifocals. I was barefoot, wearing gym shorts and a T-shirt. I'll never know what he made of me, his good-field, no-hit first baseman and sometime newsboy on his doorstep in the middle of the night, crying and sputtering hysterical terror. He opened the storm door. He squatted down and held my shoulders with his big hands. It could have been a conference between pitches in the coach's box. "Take one strike," he liked to say in the late innings. "Then wait for your pitch and drive it."

"Hey," he said. I was shaking and shivering, my teeth rattling madly in my head, my whole body convulsed with fear. "It's okay," he said. "Take it easy." His voice was a soothing instrument. I took a deep breath.

"Now tell me," he said. "What's the trouble?"

I'm not sure that I was even able to speak, but somehow, with urgent yips and tugs, like Lassie leading the way with the authorities in tow, I managed to bring him back to the house.

The lights were on and the front door was open. It was ominously quiet. I walked in slowly, Mr. Walker right behind me, dreading what we were going to find. I was imagining something like a crime scene, yellow tapes and chalk outlines of bodies splayed abjectly on the floor. But what we saw was this: My mother on her hands and knees in the back hall, with a plastic tub of soapy water and a fat yellow sponge, wiping down the floor. She was at the center of a bright circle of linoleum, a kind of sparkling spotlight in the otherwise dingy and yellow floor. The back door had been scrubbed clean, too. If not for the broken window in the door—it was still broken, I checked—I might have thought that I had imagined it all, leapt from my bed and fled nothing more than a bad dream.

Gerard was sweeping bits of broken glass and wood splinters into a neat pile with quick, energetic strokes. He may have been whistling while he worked for all I know. There was something about him suggestive at least of that sort of cheerfulness. I wanted to laugh. Where in the world did he find a broom? That's what I wanted to know. And a real dustpan, with a little leather strap so you could hang it up when you were done. In my brother's hands, they looked like props. We just didn't do housework, not anymore, not for months. We didn't sweep or dust or scrub floors or wash windows. No one bothered to chip the black crud from the stovetop. The bathroom, I don't even want to discuss. We hardly washed dishes, for chrissake. Precarious mountains of bowls and glasses and plates filled the sink and counters.

Mr. Walker stood there, smoothing down his hair, pushing his glasses up the bridge of his nose, the strangeness of it all, I suppose, slowly seeping in.

"I thought there might be trouble," he said.

"Trouble?" my mother said. "Trouble?"

Gerard held out his arm, and she pulled herself up in jerky increments, as if she were unfolding herself piece by piece, grimacing, her fingers digging desperately into the soft flesh of my brother's forearm. Mr. Walker made some fluttering motions toward assistance, but my mother waved him off. She pulled her bad leg, the right one, pure, recalcitrant dead weight, into place, and was finally upright. I was embarrassed by such a frank enactment of my mother's frailty, of her disease, by a kind of defiant intimacy it implied, but they stood there together, not in the least apologetic, my mother and brother, side by side, smiling stupidly, the happy housekeepers. She was wearing stretch pants and one of Gerard's oversized gray sweatshirt. It was what she wore nowadays, pretty much all the time, day and night. He was wearing gray sweats, too—they could have been teammates.

Mr. Walker extended his hand to my mother. "George Walker," he said.

There was an awkward pause, and then my mother's left hand swooped down suddenly and seized his hand, clamped it in a kind of vise, as if trumping his conventional handshake with some new, omnipotent sign in a game of rock, paper, scissors. She held his hand tight, and not so much shook as rattled it, like a dice cup.

"There's really no trouble," she said, and glared past Mr. Walker at me. "A simple misunderstanding," she said. "No cause for alarm."

She described something that had happened involving Mr. Hawkins, which, in her version, sounded disorderly but harmless, just grown-up mischief. Mr. Walker nodded. But I could see him studying my mother's right hand, only half-hidden at her side, puffy and purple, grotesquely swollen fingers flecked with dried blood.

Gerard emptied his dustpan into a grocery bag while Mr. Walker surveyed the place. The back hall, where he was standing, was crowded with shoes, newspapers and catalogs, a step ladder, a cardboard box full of old dog things: food dish, collar and leash, rawhide bones. In the living room, my mother's bedding—a worn bedspread and a sad-looking pillow with no case—was piled on the couch, like something on a park bench. The coffee table was littered with pop bottles, food wrappers, and empty tuna cans filled with cigarette butts. My three-speed was parked in the middle of the room, and there was an odd lot of underclothes draped from the handlebars.

"Anything I can do?" Mr. Walker said.

"Nothing," my mother said. "Not a thing."

He edged toward the front door. I wanted to offer him something, coffee, which I didn't know how to make, or a piece of cake maybe, which we didn't have. I wanted to make him stay. As he crossed the threshold, he bent down and picked something up. He held it out to me. It was a long dagger of broken glass.

"Good night," I said.

"Thank God he's a bleeder," my mother said. "The son of a bitch."

We were sitting at the kitchen table, my brother dealing graham crackers from a wax paper package like a back-room shark. "He could never stand the sight of his own blood," she said, and reached across the table to dunk a cracker in my glass of milk, which was disgusting, but I didn't say anything. She was exultant, too

42

pumped up to sleep. She was in the winner's locker room now, rehashing a big win.

It had already become a story, and it wasn't a bad one: My mother clings to the back door lock with her numb, crippled hand until my father, presumably frightened by the sight of his own blood, retreats. It was about our getting the last laugh, about the old man getting a pie in the face. It was funny because it was her disease that saved us. My mother was the unlikely hero, her holding on an uproarious triumph of comic disability, like the time she handed Gerard a hot potato, barehanded, and then watched, straight-faced, while he howled. She was like the blind gang member who inevitably ends up driving a car in the movies. Mr. Walker didn't figure in this story, nor did my own hasty departure. We all knew my father would be back, but no one said anything about that, either.

Only later, when we were lying in our bunks in the dark, my brother and I, wakeful and wary, like cellmates, he said something. "You shouldn't have," he said.

"I know," I said.

"You're a little chickenshit," he said.

"Zip it," I said.

"You'll be sorry," he said, and I knew he was right.

I lay there a long while, listening to the night sounds of the house, wondering what was coming next. Finally I fell asleep. But I must have been grinding my teeth again, because Gerard smacked me awake an hour or so later. I opened my eyes and saw him looming over me in the dark, his eyes gleaming in his soft white face, look-ing for a response. The gray light of dawn was just com-ing through the window. My jaw felt like it was vibrating.

"Thanks," I said.

CHAPTER SIX

The next morning George Walker showed up with a tape measure and a flat, red pencil. My mother was sleeping on the living room couch, and Gerard was in the basement watching television. I was headed into the kitchen for something to eat when I heard him bumping around on the back stoop, saw his big hands moving back and forth across the broken window frame.

He put his head cautiously through the window. He was wearing a white T-shirt and his coaching hat.

"Good morning," he said. He made me think of Zeke the farmhand talking to Dorothy back in Kansas the morning after. "We've got some work to do," he said.

"Yes," I said. "Absolutely."

He made a note with his pencil on a little square of white paper, and pocketed his tape measure. "I'll be right back," he said.

I could hear the sound of my mother's snoring in the living room, muffled gunfire from down the basement. I stepped outside and sat on the steps and waited. It was midmorning already. The little brown drops of dried blood on the concrete looked obscene in the light of day. My bat was lying lifeless and dejected in the basement window well.

Mr. Walker returned an hour or so later with a toolbox and a big square of glass wrapped in brown paper. He went right to work. Always the teacher and coach, he talked the whole time, describing whatever it was that he was doing aloud, breaking the job down into discrete steps—providing a kind of handyman's play-by-play. I stood by and held things for him, listening and watching. He removed a strip of wooden trim and used a pocketknife to clean out the little bits of broken glass.

He was a careful and precise worker; whatever he did, he did the right way. In his presence, I believed there was a right way. When the new pane of glass was in place and the excess putty trimmed away, Mr. Walker pulled a plastic bottle from his toolbox and sprayed the glass with bubbling blue cleaner, first one side, then the other. He took a piece of newspaper and rubbed and rubbed until it squeaked. When he was finished, that sparkling window was the cleanest thing I had ever seen. It was beautiful.

After that, the job done, Mr. Walker gathered up his things and told me that if there was anything—anything—he could do, I should let him know.

"Sure," I said. By this time my mother was stirring— I could hear her moving around in the living room. I didn't think she'd be glad to see Mr. Walker again so soon. The last thing I wanted was another scene.

"Promise?" he said.

"Promise," I said, and raised my hand stupidly, the way I thought a Boy Scout would do it.

"We're getting out of here," my mother told me. She was dragging a battered brown suitcase from the front hall closet. Her hand was wrapped in gauze, but it still looked awful, her fingers all purple and swollen.

"Where?" I said. "Where are we going?"

"A motel," she said. "Just for a day or two." She said we needed to get away—"cool our heels" was her phrase, which I kind of liked, that edge of danger and glamorous criminality.

"Okay," I said, and went upstairs and started packing my gym bag. Gerard whined a little, he had unspecified plans, things to do, people to see, but I don't think he really wanted to stick around anymore than I did. He threw a few things in a grocery bag—underwear, magazines, a pack of Marlboros—and changed into a relatively clean shirt.

I called a cab from the corner booth, and we waited on the front steps. Mrs. Gunsher was crouched on her boulevard across the street, going through the motions of pulling weeds, taking it all in. She must have heard the hullabaloo the night before and was waiting to see what was going to happen next. We were her own personal soap opera.

My mother lit a cigarette and took a long drag. "Next time," she said, real loud, "he's coming after nosy neighbors. They'd better watch out."

A big Checker showed up a few minutes later with a

bald, grandfatherly driver, who was extraordinarily polite and solicitous about my mother. He stowed her suitcase in the trunk, took her by the elbow and gently eased her into the backseat, held her cane while she adjusted her legs, and asked again and again if she was all right. Gerard and I waited at the curb and watched. For just a moment, it was as if I could see her, really see her—her limp, her bandaged hand, her cane. She was someone who needed help.

We rode in silence, the three of us shoulder to shoulder in the backseat, watching the numbers on the meter, self-conscious and embarrassed. I knew that we looked exactly like what we were, domestic refugees, a ragtag family on the run.

The Thunderbird was just off 494, near the airport, right next to Metropolitan Stadium where the Twins played. There was a big totem pole out front, painted in vivid blue and red, a two-story stack of wide-eyed, grinning hawks and owls. My mother paid the cabby with a few crumpled bills and a handful of change she fished from her coin purse.

While she leaned on the front desk and checked us in, Gerard and I looked around the lobby. The walls were full of flattened animal skins—teeth bared, legs splayed—looking like a flock of crazy flying mammals. In a glass case, there was a seven-foot stuffed grizzly with long yellow claws and slightly crossed glass eyes, reared up on his hind legs, its mouth open, looking fierce in a dopey sort of half-hearted way, like Gentle Ben. Everywhere you looked, there was some kind of native knick-knackery—feathered pipes and tomahawks, head-dresses, canoe paddles.

We sat down on a black leather couch outside the Hall of Tribes.

"Dad told me he saw Koufax and Drysdale here during the '65 series," I said.

"Here?"

"In the bar," I said. "After game two."

"He's full of shit," Gerard said.

"How do you know?"

"Did he get you an autograph?"

"Maybe he didn't want to bother them."

"He's full of shit," Gerard said.

My mother waved us over. She had two keys in her hand and a big smile on her face. "Two forty-nine," she said. "In the back."

Now I know full well that motel rooms are supposed to be sad and sordid places, but I'm sorry, I loved ours, everything about it. I loved the big color TV. I loved the bathroom—the paper seal across the toilet bowl, miniature bars of soap and vials of shampoo, unlimited hot water and mountains of towels. The DO NOT DISTURB sign hanging on the doorknob. I loved the king-size beds and the bear-and-bison art hanging on the walls. I loved our view of the Met Stadium parking lot.

It rained on and off the rest of the day, so while my mother camped out in the room, Gerard and I headed down to the indoor pool. We didn't have regulation bathing suits, but we made do, me with gym shorts, my brother in a pair of khaki cut-offs and a white T-shirt. There was no lifeguard on duty, so except for one older woman in a black one-piece and pearl-diver goggles swimming laps, we had the place pretty much to ourselves. We dove for pennies, held our noses and cannon-balled off the low board, batted an underinflated beach ball back and forth.

In the pool, Gerard seemed sleek and playful, like a big sea lion—awkward and blubbery on land, but in the water, surprisingly swift and graceful. He was a good swimmer, underwater especially, capable of traveling great distances along the bottom. Sometimes I'd lose sight of him at the far end of the pool and the next thing I knew, he'd have me by the ankles. He'd come up, clear his nose, shake back his hair, take a deep breath, and do it again. He'd always loved swimming pools, water slides, hot tubs. It had to do with personal physics, I imagined. In the water, he must have felt freer, lighter—just like on skates—less oppressed by gravity and friction and the burden of his own considerable mass.

When my brother toweled off and ducked into the men's locker room for a smoke, I stayed in and floated on my back awhile with my eyes closed, my nose full of the clean sting of chlorine, listening to the warm splash and lap of the pool, the hypnotic hum of pump and filter, a faint, muted rumble of thunder from somewhere outside. I thought about my father at the door—the broken glass, his hand reaching blindly for the lock, all that blood. It seemed real to me now but distant, the images had hardened already into memory, my private newsreel footage.

Later we fooled around with the stationary bike and rowing machine we found in the exercise room. I did maybe a dozen sit-ups on an elevated board while my brother held my feet. There was a bench and a barbell in there, too, and I spotted Gerard while he did some lifting. My brother was jiggly fat, but he was strong, too, especially his upper body. He had the soft, massy power of a sumo wrestler. He put all the loose weights he could find on the bar and attempted one single spectacular press. He stalled halfway up, his arms quivering in rapid spasms, his face heart-attack red, his eyes wide and panicked-looking. Afraid that he was going to get crushed and pinned there, I reached for the bar, but he shook his head and made an angry growl. He took a deep breath then, let loose one explosive grunt, and raised the bar the rest of the way in one fast jerk. He held it there for a few seconds, his arms locked, breathing hard. He was making a point, I guess, trying to prove something, I don't know what, maybe to me, maybe just to himself.

We ate dinner in the Bow and Arrow coffee shop. My mother had said she wasn't hungry but insisted that my brother and I go. Gerard asked her how we were supposed to pay.

"Charge it to the room," she said.

"Can you do that?" I asked. "Really?"

"Just sign the check," my mother said. "Show 'em your key."

The hostess greeted us, all smiles and genial deference, as if we really were gentlemen and not just a couple of wet-haired kids. She seated us at a table right next to a teepee in the middle of the room, a kind of animal-skin pup tent decorated with feathers and cornstalks, which housed an artificial fireplace, the orange glow of an electric flame flickering beneath a pile of birch logs.

We ordered half-pound cheeseburgers, sides of fries and onion rings, malts, and Cokes. Because no money was going to change hands, it felt free. We ordered apple pie for dessert, with ice cream. My brother polished his off in a couple of big bites and started eyeing my piece. Sometimes I think that the more he ate, the hungrier he got.

"What if you could *live* at the Thunderbird?" I said.

"Nobody lives at the Thunderbird," my brother said.

"What if you could?"

"You'd get sick of it," Gerard said.

"Not me," I said.

We went outside after that and walked over to have a look at the stadium. It was just misting now, but puddles had formed in the pavement's low spots, which, now, in the dark, looked black and oily. There were big poles scattered across the Met parking lot, set in concrete, like light standards, meant to help you remember where you left your car; each one was decorated with the emblem of an American League team: grinning

Chief Wahoo, the Cleveland Indian; Detroit's snarling Tiger; the winged cleats of the California Angels. We zigzagged our way across the lot, dodging puddles. I touched the base of the poles as we passed them, just for luck, and with the stadium in plain view across the expansive lot—the lights, the colored panels on its face, the ramps leading up to the second and third decks, the yellow foul poles, the scoreboard—I broke into a trot. It was like approaching the Emerald City in Oz.

The Twins were on the road, but still, this was a big-league ballpark. I'd only been to a handful of games in my life, Knothole Gang days with my baseball buddies. Somebody's mom would drop off a station wagon full of us in the morning. We'd sit in the rickety right-field bleachers usually, where we'd watch the guys in the vis-itor's bullpen goof off and we'd holler at their reliev-ers—threats, flattery, jokes, anything to get them to throw us a ball, or just acknowledge us, which they never did.

We walked along the perimeter of the stadium on the third base side. Before a game there'd be vendors there, hawking scorecards and yearbooks, scalpers standing silently with fat fists full of tickets fanned out like poker hands, dads distributing tickets to their kids before heading through the gate. Now, the place was dark and deserted, eerily quiet. We tried the doors on the tickets booths and rattled the chains on the press gate. Every-thing was locked, of course.

"Man," I said. "I wish."

"They don't even take tickets after the fourth inning," Gerard said. "Did you know that? They open the gates. We could just walk in and then work our way down to the empty boxes."

I knew that a lot of the fat cats with season tickets didn't even show up. Fans who came late and left early baffled and irritated me—I mean, why bother?—but no-shows were beyond my comprehension, beneath my contempt. Even as I imagined sitting in their empty seats, I hated them.

We walked down a narrow paved road behind the center-field bleachers in back of the batter's eye. It was spooky back there, like an alley in a bad neighborhood, full of shadows and imaginary menace.

Around the bend, I spotted the relief pitcher's car, parked in the bullpen, a little black convertible.

"On Fan Appreciation Day," I told Gerard, "they're gonna give that car away."

"Who cares?" he said.

"I'd take it," I said. "It's a nice car."

"Now it's a nice car," Gerard said. "Wait till September. It's gonna be a beater, a high-mileage piece of shit."

I hung on the Hurricane fence and stood on my toes. I could see a thick black hose, a wheelbarrow, a couple of metal watering cans, big bags of what might have been fertilizer. What I wanted to see was the field. I wanted to get just a glimpse of green, but in the dark, from where I was standing, there was no way.

Back at the Thunderbird, Gerard got some change, bought a can of Mountain Dew, and settled in at a

bank of pay phones in the lobby. He was hoping
to connect with one of his licensed friends, somebody
with a car who could take him away. I would have
liked him to stick around, go for a midnight swim
maybe, but I knew that that wasn't his idea of a big
night.

I opened a directory at the next phone and looked up
George Walker's number. I'd missed practice that night
and thought I ought to apologize. He answered on the
first ring. He sounded apprehensive, like he was expecting bad news. "I'm sorry," I told him.

"Don't worry about it," he said. "No problem."

"It won't happen again," I said.

"Are you all right?" he asked. "Is your family all
right?"

It threw me off a little, who that was exactly. I didn't
think of my brother and mother and me as constituting
a family.

"Yes," I said. "I think so."

When I hung up, Gerard was still on the other phone.
I nosed around in the gift shop and watched him
through the glass. With his back turned, feeding the
phone dimes, a cigarette cupped furtively in his hand, he
looked sad and desperate and a little scary, like somebody you'd rather not sit next to on the bus. I thought
about buying a postcard—they had a nice shot of the
grizzly in the lobby, an aerial view of the hotel and stadium—but who would I send it to?

Finally, I got tired of waiting. I tapped Gerard on the
shoulder and pointed up, in the direction of our room.

He nodded impatiently. "What about Russell?" he was saying. "His parents are out of town, right?"

When I stepped into what I thought was an empty elevator, I smelled the man—he was leaning in the front corner, propped up there, like a fighter between rounds—before I saw him. Even before I smelled him, or before I knew I smelled him, I felt scared—some kind of neurological lightning before thunder. My heart just started beating like crazy, and my legs went wobbly. He made some noise—a kind of throaty bark—and I turned then and saw him. He was just a standard-issue drunk, reeking of booze; his face had that red, rashy, scrubbed-raw quality, with dark, purplish, bruised-looking patches around the eyes. He was wearing a blue blazer and a white shirt. He had a big smile on his face.

"Where's the party?" he said.

I couldn't think of an answer so I didn't say anything. The man was harmless. He was probably a salesman up from Austin or Mankato for a convention. But the more he smiled, the worse I felt. I could hear the glass breaking again. The elevator moved so slowly, I thought for a second that it was stuck. When the doors finally did open, I stepped out fast and headed down the hall. I heard the man saying something, but I didn't look back.

Back in the room, I felt relieved to see my mother. She looked like a familiar landmark, reassuringly substantial. She was sitting on the edge of one of the beds, looking pleased and relaxed, her bare feet propped on a kind of makeshift footstool—a pile of pillows and folded towels. The television was playing and she had a room service tray next to her—cheese, crackers, a cut glass dish full of melon and strawberries.

"Are they cool?" I asked.

"What?" she said.

"Your heels," I said.

She glanced in the direction of her feet, as if she were inspecting them. They were puffy and painful-looking, the swelling somehow related to her MS. "Not yet," she said. "But they're getting there."

I stretched out on the other bed—it was like a trampoline, that vast and springy—and we watched highlights of the Twins game on the ten o'clock news. They were in New York, beating the Yankees. Killebrew and Oliva had both homered earlier in the game, and Dean Chance, chosen as the starting pitcher in the All-Star game, had his good stuff. The Twins had gotten off to a slow start—playing .500 ball through June, stuck in the middle of the pack—but were finally coming around. They were in second place, a game behind the White Sox, and I was starting to like their chances.

The Yankees were pathetic that season, which took some getting used to. Mantle was playing hurt. Clete Boyer, the slick-fielding third baseman, a favorite of mine, was gone now, replaced in the line-up by Charlie Smith, a Mets castoff, a player who got traded so often I used to think that there were at least two Charlie Smiths in the league, both third basemen, both distinguished only by their crewcuts and weak arms. The

whole team seemed to be composed of impostors—
Reuben Amaro, Horace Clarke, Dooley Womack.
These guys were a sorry bunch, but they were Yankees,
and I loved beating them.

My mother used a plastic knife to spread something
on a cracker and told me to help myself. I picked a
strawberry from her fruit cup, threw it gently in the air,
and positioned my open mouth underneath. It was a
lunchroom trick I'd recently mastered. I caught it square
on my tongue.

"Not bad," my mother said. "But I bet you can't do
it again."

She lifted a melon ball from her dish and tossed it at
me. I snagged it. Before I could swallow, she threw me
another. She kept throwing them at me, one piece of
fruit after another, faster and harder, with less and less
of an arc on each one, more like line drives than pop-
ups, a little wild too—she was doing this left-handed,
after all—until I had a mouth full of melon, rivers of red
juice running down my chin. It wasn't a food fight so
much as a gangland assassination. I'd done something
like four or five in row before she bounced one off my
nose.

My brother walked in at that point, looking surly and
flushed, and all of a sudden the weather in the room
changed. I could sense somehow that he'd done something he shouldn't have. He'd stolen something, ingested
something, I don't know what, except that he looked
hot with secrecy and guilt. He had a handful of vending-
machine food—potato chips, peanut butter cups, a

Kit-Kat. His plans had obviously not materialized and he seemed resentfully resigned to staying in.

"What are you looking at?" he said.

We were laughing, but not at him. He wouldn't have believed me if I told him that, though, and I couldn't talk anyway, my mouth was full.

My mother made noises in her sleep. When I awoke in the middle of the night, that's what I heard, a kind of rhythmic moaning, a tortured rise and fall, a guttural song with no words, just the music of her misery. I'd fallen asleep with the television on—the last thing I remember was the sound of Perry Mason's voice, relentlessly grilling some guy on the stand—my mother in one bed, my brother and I on opposite sides of the other. I'd been dreaming about the guy on the elevator—he was asking me questions, a rapid-fire interrogation of some kind, grinning like a maniac, edging closer and closer to where I stood paralyzed, unable to move or speak. Gerard was making noise now, too, not snoring exactly, his breathing was just hard, labored, and I wondered what he was dreaming about—lifting weights? I lay there awhile, wide awake suddenly, feeling twitchy and anxious.

I knew that my mother's whole right side was numb, which was feeling nothing really, a kind of weird, bloated nothing, I imagined, like Novocain maybe, maybe a tingling nothing, like frostbite. So why was she moaning? I wondered sometimes how bad she was going to get, how soon. I wondered what was worse than numb.

The *World Book* described the disease as a kind of guerrilla war—attacks on certain areas of the brain and spinal cord. I used to study the encyclopedia's transparent five-page overlay of the human body, searching in vain for some clue, maybe just a way to understand the damage. But underneath it all, once I flipped past all the over systems—skeletal and muscular, digestive, respiratory—the nervous system was a disappointingly basic wiring diagram, a bunch of beige-colored bundles plugged into the brain's furrowed meat.

I got up and went in the bathroom, peeled the plastic from a fresh glass and took a long cold drink of water. I came out then and sat on the edge of the bed. My mother was quiet now, and even though I couldn't really see her—she was just a shape in the dark—I knew somehow that she was awake.

"It's gonna be okay," my mother said. Her voice was soft, but there was an edge of impatient argument to it, as if we'd already being going back and forth awhile about this. She sounded a little pissed, is what I'm saying.

"All right," I said. "It's gonna be okay."

I was hoping she might say some more—tell me what "it" was, for example, that was going to be okay, explain the happy chain of circumstances by which this would be accomplished—but of course she never did. Pretty soon her breathing got regular and she was moaning in her sleep again, sounding unspeakably sad and exhausted.

Check-out time was at eleven o'clock, and we lingered in the room as long as possible the next morning, getting our money's worth. My mother had fired up the little coffeemaker and was on her second cup. Gerard had returned from the lobby with a plate full of complimentary pastries and a newspaper.

I stuffed a few towels in my bag, a couple of small ones, hand towels, and one big bath towel, all decorated with a big T and the image of a two-headed bird. Maybe I was under the impression that there was nothing wrong with that, that it wasn't stealing—it was just what you did, it was expected. My mother saw me, and she didn't say anything. I tossed in some more stuff—soap, an ashtray, a couple of pens, and a notepad, and then, the little green Gideon Bible. I did, I really did, I pinched a Bible.

It's impossible to say just how dismal, how sorry and shabby, our house looked when we returned to it. Gerard turned the key and shouldered the front door open—it stuck in the summer—and we stepped inside. It smelled, for one thing, sour and stale, like old, wet laundry, like milk spilled in the fridge and yesterday's bacon grease. It worried me a little that I was noticing it only now, that I must have grown accustomed to it. What did *I* smell like?

My mother sat down heavily on the couch in the living room. Gerard went downstairs and turned on the television. It was like we'd never left. I wandered around the downstairs for a while, circling through the living room and dining rooms, down the front hall and past the back door and the new window, into the kitchen, trying to figure out just where the bad smell was coming from.

CHAPTER SEVEN

The next day, on a humid July afternoon, when I came
down the street with my bag of newspapers, straining
and sweating, the strap cutting my shoulder, George
Walker was sitting on his front steps, fiddling around
with a fishing reel, arranging tiny parts on a white hand-
kerchief. I had the feeling somehow that he was waiting
for me.

"Hey, Mr. Walker," I said, and handed him his
paper, headline up. There were air strikes north of
Hanoi, riots in New Haven.

"Thanks," he said, and glanced at the front page
photo of LBJ hanging a medal of honor around a bristly
marine sergeant's neck. TOWERING VALOR, the cutline
read.

"I was wondering," he said, "whether you might like
to make some money." He had some yardwork that
needed to be done, odd jobs, mowing, a little trimming,
some weeding, maybe washing the car. A few hours a
week. "You interested?" he said.

"Sure," I said. "I'm interested."

I showed up on Saturday morning, and Mr. Walker put me to work. It became a weekly routine, and I loved it. My brother, who would just be settling in front of the television with a bowl of cereal and a carton of milk, thought I was crazy. "Let him cut his own grass," he said. He didn't understand. Mr. Walker had great tools, for one thing, everything you needed to do the job right. A shiny red power mower with an automatic choke. A dangerously sharp hand trimmer, rakes and spades with real heft, tempered like swords. A chamois for drying off the car.

George Walker instructed me in the rituals of lawn and garden, common sense and good practice reduced to formula, which I found reassuring. You washed the car from the top down. Every time out, you checked the oil in the mower, and once a month you rinsed the spongy filter with gasoline. You blew the grass out, so it wouldn't pile in the middle of the yard.

I washed his car every week, a green Mercury wagon, which, in fact, was never that dirty. I swept out the floor with a whisk broom and touched up the upholstery with a damp cloth. I washed down the outside with a bucket of soapy water and a big sponge, scrubbed the bugs from the windshield and the tar from the fenders, and rinsed slowly with the hose, watching the water cascade in sheets from the car and then bead up on the well-waxed hood.

I usually spent the rest of the time cutting grass and pulling weeds, and there was a certain satisfying clarity involved in that work, too. Unlike our dull and rusty push mower at home, which didn't so much cut as bend the grass, which always clogged and got stuck, Mr. Walker's Toro cut an unambiguous swath through the tallest grass. I liked pushing the mower on the long straightaway in his backyard, following the well-defined path of my wheels, eyeing the shrinking rectangle of uncut grass in the center. In the flower beds, there were rosebushes and there were weeds. Nothing doubtful about it at all. You pulled and hoed and raked and watered, and afterward, it looked like it was supposed to. And when you were done, you were done.

While I worked, Mr. Walker busied himself around the yard, pruning, spraying his beloved roses with a fine white powder, moving the sprinkler.

Afterward, once I had raked and swept the sidewalks, tied the bags of clippings, washed the mower and stowed the tools in the garage, he asked me in for a Coke.

I wiped my feet and sat cautiously in a spinning vinyl kitchen chair, polite and self-conscious, but fanatically observant. The kitchen was always neat, eerily so, it seemed to me, who thought I detected his dead wife's order preserved and maintained. There was a full set of colorful fruit magnets—banana, apple, strawberry, grapes—arranged on the fridge in a perfect line, holding up nothing at all. There were place mats on the table all day long, a fancy dish of layered chocolate mints and a silver bowl of mixed nuts, always full. There was a message pad hanging next to the wall phone and a pen attached with purple yarn.

I was too shy to say very much, but Mr. Walker was a teacher after all, whose job it was to lecture. He did most of the talking. Sometimes we just looked out the back window together in silent admiration, watched the sprinkler moving back and forth over the freshly cut lawn. When we did converse, it was mostly about base-ball, our Twins, the only subject I really knew anything about. I discovered that underneath Mr. Walker's base-ball smarts and long experience, his conviction that Boswell needed another pitch, that Allison had lost a step, he was really a fan, just like me, a true believer. When it came to baseball, we were both optimists. If they can just sweep the Sox this weekend, I would say. If Killebrew's hamstring holds up, if Quilici comes through, and Mr. Walker would nod and fill my glass and it all seemed almost plausible.

But if he asked me anything, however indirectly, about what went on at my house, if he even so much as hinted in that direction, I clammed up, lied, got forget-ful and stupid. I was a good soldier. "Fine," I would say. "Fine." And change the subject.

He paid me on the way out, generously, in cash. He would stuff some bills in my hand, always nice and fresh, and I would say thank you, and not look until I was down the block and out of sight. I squirreled the money away at home in a cigar box at the bottom of my closet and took it out from time to time only to count and admire it, always the collector, fingering those crisp bills with their solemn portraits, Washington, Lincoln, a few Hamiltons, like rare stock certificates, too precious to circulate.

. . .

I started riding with Mr. Walker to our ballgames. I liked sitting next to him in the front seat of his car, the team's score book and a boxed game ball between us, his big black compass bobbing around on top of the rearview mirror. We listened to WCCO on the radio, Good Neighbor to the Great Northwest, the Twins' sponsor. When Sid Hartman came on with his daily one-minute interview "Today's Sports Hero"—almost always a Twins player—Mr. Walker would reach down and turn up the volume a little. I'd take the ball from its box and rub it up. Big league umpires took the sheen off new balls with special mud from the Potomac river, I'd read, treating dozens before every game. I'd grip the ball as if I were going to throw it, first with the seams, then against them, turn my wrist in for an imaginary curveball, out for a screwball. Mr. Walker had told me that Carl Hubbell had thrown so many screwballs—he called it a fade-away, but it was the same thing—that late in life his hand would fall naturally at his side with his palm out.

We would always be the first to arrive. Mr. Walker would unlock the groundskeeper's shed, while I lined up bats and helmets behind the backstop. Together we prepped the diamond. We raked the infield, pegged bases, filled the holes on the mound and around home plate. On wet days, we dug little sluices and spread wheelbarrows full of sand in order to make the puddles disappear. Last, and best, we would chalk the field: Mr. Walker held the string while I took the slow, bowlegged walk down the baseline with the spreader, poking it every once in a while with a stick to keep the chalk flowing. It wasn't necessary, but most of the time I did the batter's boxes, too. I loved it, the art of the straight line and the square corner.

When the other guys started to arrive, we played catch and shagged flies and Mr. Walker threw batting practice. It was a little strange being coached by him now that he'd seen me crying on his front steps, knowing that he'd been in my house—not good, not bad, just different.

Mr. Walker was, well, Mr. Walker. On the ball field, he was always at ease, perfectly consistent. He batted me seventh, same as always, which was low in the order for a first baseman, but right where I belonged. The fact that he had been to our house and fixed our window or that I washed his car didn't seem to enter into it at all. He hit infield and coached third and told us to run everything out. He clapped his hands and talked it up.

That summer we kept winning—six in a row before we lost a heartbreaker in South St. Paul when Eddie Doyle walked in the winning run. Mr. Walker told us to keep an even keel, don't get too pumped up, don't get down, not too high, not too low. It was going to be a long season.

I packed up bats and balls and bases and stowed them in the back of Mr. Walker's wagon. When he'd drop me off, he let the car idle at the curb while I gathered up my cleats and my mitt. He seemed to be inspecting the house, and whether he was or not, I imagined it through his eyes and saw how bad it looked—the yard and flower beds full of weeds, a sheet draped over the window in my bedroom. I felt shame, warm and insistent, on me like an allergic reaction, a kind of angry rash.

After a while, Mr. Walker started to give me things. One gray, drizzly morning, he brought out a black windbreaker for me. It was some kind of warm-up jacket. METRO CHAMPS was emblazoned across the back, COACH stitched across the front in white thread. "Put this on," he said. It was lined, practically new, good and warm. I pushed the sleeves up and wore it while I trimmed the back hedge. I kept it on as we sat at the kitchen table afterward, and Mr. Walker sized me up.

"That fits you," he said, tugging at the shoulders. I was swimming in it. "Just right," he said. He said, "You keep it. I never wear it. I've got closets full of jackets I don't know what to do with."

The way he talked, I was doing him a big favor by taking it. "Sure," I said. "Thanks."

Later, he gave me a catcher's mitt and a set of rubber bases that he found in the garage, a tennis racket, a half-set of Sam Snead golf clubs and a dozen practice balls. He got into the habit of sending me home with a fresh can of Coke. "One for the road," he liked to say. One day he caught me fiddling with a fat, four-color ballpoint pen that was lying on the kitchen table and insisted that I take it. "Pens, pens," he said, "the house is full of pens." I became wary of letting my gaze linger too long on any object for fear that he would make me take it home with me.

And then one Saturday as I was headed out the door, almost as an after-thought, he pulled a shoe box from the back closet and presented it to me. I sat back down and lifted the lid, a little scared. I could smell rubber, I swear. It was a pair of leather sneakers, brand new, Adidas Superstars, the kind that, back then, only Mr. Walker and the varsity basketball players wore. My own sneakers were ratty, falling-apart specials pulled long ago from a Target bargain bin.

"Maybe you can get some use from these," Mr. Walker said. "They don't fit me quite right."

"Thank you, Mr. Walker," I said. "Thank you." He made an awkward, downward gesture with his hand, a small, shy wave. He turned and busied himself at the sink, wiping down the immaculate countertops with a wet rag while I tried on the shoes.

The thing is, they were my size, not his, not even close to his. I knew damn well they were no castoffs. He bought them especially for me. But I also knew not to question the lies of adults, no matter how transparent. Besides, these were no ordinary shoes. I stood and looked down at my feet, laced in fresh white leather, adorned with those jaunty black stripes, and I felt different, fast and nimble, a little shifty.

When I came bouncing through the front door in my new shoes, pivoted with a squeak on the hall tile, and made an imaginary jump shot into the living room, my mother took notice. "No," she said. She was slumped on the couch, having a smoke. "Take them back," she said. No need to ask questions, she understood the situation perfectly. "Tell Mr. Fixit no thanks."

"Mom," I said. "I need them."

She didn't care. "Take them back," she said. "Or I will."

I felt angry, impotent disbelief, something hot and highly charged, something like hatred, for my mother and her granite opposition to what I wanted. I understood why my father broke things.

"No," I said. "I won't." There was silence then. We were both surprised, I think.

"It isn't fair," I said.

She laughed. It was an angry, acid laugh, the poisoned betrayal of her whole life contained and concentrated in it, like a deadly, bitter bouillon cube of the blackest humor.

She made for her cane, pulled it from the floor beside her, and started to hoist herself awkwardly. Her hands were stiff and awkward, crudely primitive, like flippers. It seemed to me then that she was not so much getting sicker as becoming transformed, slowly and inevitably, into something monstrous. She was so full of theatrical determination and malign resolution that I knew right then that the game was over. There was no way I was going to win this one.

I unlaced the shoes and pulled them off. I laid them carefully back in the box, covered them with tissue. I slipped into my old shoes and headed down the street.

Mr. Walker opened the door. "Here," I said, and put

the box in his hands. He looked down at me, puzzled, blinking owlishly behind his black glasses.

"My mother says no," I told him. "I can't." And he nodded slowly, a little sadly, as if he understood.

CHAPTER EIGHT

Somehow, in the middle of an August heat wave, we acquired a car, a frown-faced Plymouth Valiant. I came home one day from working at Mr. Walker's, shirtless and sweaty, complimentary Coke in hand, and there it was, parked out front.

"Look out the window," my mother said.

"What?" I said, and held the cold can to my forehead. "It's a car."

"It's *our* car," she said, and grinning, held up a key chain, dangling it, like a hypnotist's charm.

She wouldn't tell me where she got it. "None of your business," she said.

It crossed my mind that it was hot, that she'd stolen it. Probably she had just done some talking to somebody, a banker, or Charlie O'Connell, or maybe even my father. She could be slick on the phone, a master of plead and thank you. When she wanted something, she had a way of describing our situation in such a way that, even though truthful in all the particulars, it always sounded to me like she was scamming.

The car wasn't that old, but it was beat. The tires were bald. There was tape on the upholstery, and the backseat, where I sat most of the time, gave off a lingering fetid odor, stale beer and something else, rankly human. It burned oil and leaked fluids. To start the car, you had to lift the hood and clamp a pliers to the battery's corroded cables while someone else turned the key. It was a two-man cooperative operation, like the Wright brothers at Kitty Hawk. But the thing ran, that's what counted, that's all that mattered. It ran.

My mother loved to drive, and no wonder. For her, driving must have been like a crippled child's dreams of dancing, a reprieve, a gasoline-powered remission. Behind the wheel, she seemed most intensely alive. I can still see her: the front seat pulled all the way forward, her left foot on the accelerator—barefoot in summer, wearing something soft and roomy in cold weather, slippers, moccasins—both hands gripping the wheel, and a look of alert pleasure on her face. She liked to go fast. Gerard's buddy Danny Sellers saw her lay rubber in the school parking lot one afternoon and called her Leadfoot ever after, even to her face, and she loved it.

My father returned just a few days after we got the car. This time, we were ready for him. We didn't know it, but we had a plan. He turned up after closing time one stifling night and started pounding on the back door. It was suffocating upstairs, so Gerard and I had dragged blankets downstairs and made up beds on the living room floor. That's where we were, camped out, my mother on the couch, when we heard him.

"Open the goddamn door," he said.

Gerard and I were up and dressed fast as firefighters. My mother already had the front door propped open and the car keys in her hand.

"Let me in," my father was saying. "For chrissake."

Now he sounded only a little annoyed, impatient, mildly irritated, as if he'd just forgotten his keys and been accidentally locked out. My mother hobbled down the walk and I opened the driver's side door for her and slipped in the backseat. Gerard grabbed the pliers and opened the hood. By the time my father figured it out— heard doors slamming and the motor running and looked to the street—we were already rolling. He took a few tentative steps in our direction. He looked so bewildered, betrayed really—we were cheating, how dare we?—that I almost felt sorry for him, and my mother, who couldn't resist, gave the horn a couple of short, cheery beeps as we pulled away.

"Hot damn," Gerard said. "We did it."

Fact is there just weren't many places for a crippled mother and her two boys to go at two in the morning, not that much to do. We stopped at SuperAmerica and loaded up on snacks. Gerard and I handed a bag of chips back and forth, traded gumdrops, my blacks for his greens. We drove and ate and argued a little. We played twenty questions. Gerard punched the buttons on the radio. Having fallen asleep without knowing what the White Sox did, I wanted to hear baseball scores, but my brother favored rock and roll. Gerard propped his feet on the dash, and I stuck my head out the window, like a dog, enjoying the breeze. It was like an impromptu vacation, with no Triptik and no destination.

My mother followed her own favorite routes, traveled an unconscious circuit, automatic and repetitive as a caged animal's, a kind of geographic enactment of her life, her fears and desires. We drove down dark side streets on the West Side, where my mother grew up, Robie, Stryker, Bidwell, through Cherokee Park, eerily empty at night, overlooking the river, where, she used to tell us, hobos made camp, ate from tin cans, and threatened passersby with switchblades and sharpened screwdrivers. I thought I saw something that night, the glint of a weapon, a figure in the shadows.

We drove over the Wabasha Bridge into downtown St. Paul, the streets deserted save for a few diehard, jacked-up hot rodders, who sometimes would return our thumbs-up at the red lights. We drove past my father's office building, where he took me one memorable Saturday and let me type and spin in his secretary's chair and look through the glossies in his dog-bite files while he murmured into a Dictaphone. We drove past Mitch's and Gallivan's, where he drank, past Miller Hospital, where my brother and I were born, where my mother was diagnosed. We cruised past the Pioneer Press building, where the rumbling delivery trucks were being loaded with the newspapers my brother was supposed to deliver in a few hours, then past Mickey's Diner, open all night, lit up, a garish yellow train car parked on Seventh Street, the counter filled with tantalizingly disreputable-looking nighthawks.

"Please," we begged. "Some eggs, a doughnut. We're starving." The women were prostitutes, my brother had informed me, and I was dying to see one, up close.

We drove up the dizzying incline of the Ramsey Hill, past the James J. Hill house and down Summit Avenue, where F. Scott Fitzgerald used to live, a street lined with doomed elm trees and ornate street lamps, crowded with mansions and carriage houses, brick and ivy covered, with turrets and towers, like castles and haunted houses. There was one church after another, including St. Luke's, where my parents were married. We drove north on Snelling Avenue, past Midway Stadium and the fairgrounds, and then beyond the city limits, farther and farther down dark, mostly unmarked county roads. My mother didn't see well at night—she squinted something awful—but she just flipped on the high beams and kept her foot on the gas. She drifted over the center line and never slowed at the blinking ambers. Other drivers could yield to her, that was her attitude.

I saw the headlights of the other cars and I wondered about the people inside, all the people we had seen, more than you might think, making their nocturnal rounds, derelicts and drunks, out prowling and racing, lonely night owls and all manner of lowlife, hanging out, killing time, every variation of desperation. We were desperate, too. You had to be. But tooling down some dark two-lane highway at sixty miles per, the dash glowing green and the radio blasting, I didn't feel scared or envious of the good people snug in their beds. I felt free somehow. I felt alive.

Finally, we got lost. To this day, I have no idea where we were. We were way beyond the neat suburban neighborhoods now, the blocks and blocks of boxy postwar aluminum-sided houses, beyond the fast-food strips, beyond the golf courses and industrial parks, into some in-between region that was neither country nor city, not so much undeveloped as ignored, no houses and no barns, just ditches and telephone poles.

After a while, we came across a fence-lined enclosure, official and secret, like some kind of compound or base. The sign said KEEP OUT, but the gate was open. My mother turned in. Gerard killed the radio, and I rolled my window down. We all leaned forward a little. We could hear a soft, rhythmic sound, fluid music, like a waterfall. We pulled up to a miniature stop sign and followed yellow arrows painted on the blacktopped road. There were a few low-slung clapboard buildings, and beyond them, black water gleaming in the moonlight in long perfect rectangles, like an endless, crazy network of swimming pools. It was like a fish hatchery, only as we got closer, I could see that these pools were bubbling, churning, white with chemical froth. The air was filled with an evil, sulfurous odor. We followed the winding road deeper inside and the smell got worse and worse. Eventually we figured it out: this concrete, foul-smelling Venice was a sewage treatment center. My mother made a quick U-turn, we rolled up the windows, and with the smell of chlorinated shit still burning in our nostrils, we headed out, looking for the road that would take us home.

By the time we pulled up to the house, the sun was coming up. Gerard and I had fallen asleep in the car, and we were both stiff and tired, greasy and mean. The only sign of my father was a couple of burnt butts I found on the back steps. My brother said that if I helped him with his papers he would buy me a glazed dough-nut at Ed's.

"Two," I said. "And a bear claw." He needed me, we both knew it.

"Little asshole," he said.

CHAPTER NINE

Early one morning late in the summer, I woke to some strange noises downstairs, banging and clattering, the rush of water, some murmuring. It was coming from the kitchen. It was loud as hell, but sort of methodical, not quite destructive.

I found my mother standing at the sink, up to her elbows in soapsuds, the taps wide open, a long line of gleaming pots and pans drying on the counter. There was soapy water pooling at her feet, a big grin on her face. She started singing. It was five A.M. *Good morning, Mr. Zip, Zip, Zip.* I knew what it meant: My mother was in remission.

It had happened a couple of times before, never for very long, an inexplicable, unsought—and tantalizingly temporary—respite from her symptoms. It was like grace, with a due date. For as long as her remission lasted, she had a return of some kind of sensation. She tried to explain it to me once. The feeling, she said, wasn't real—it was some crazy kind of misfiring, synthetic neural music—but it was feeling, which was better than nothing. She asked whether I understood, and I said that I did.

It was like having company—an unruly, boisterous, and utterly charming houseguest who arrives unexpectedly with a suitcase full of impractical gifts, turns the house upside-down, and then disappears as quickly as he came, leaving only sad silence behind. It was fun while it lasted.

We cleaned the kitchen together that morning, my mother working the steel wool, me drying. Even Gerard joined in eventually, sort of noncommittally at first, scraping halfheartedly at the stovetop with a spatula. Something interesting was happening, and he wanted to be a part of it.

My mother emptied the cupboard under the sink then, and distributed cleaning products—rags and buckets, Ajax and Mr. Clean, brushes and sponges—like a sheriff arming a posse. Between the three of us, we must have sprayed every available surface with scrubbing bubbles. Our work was hit-and-miss—nobody bothered to clean behind the stove, for example, none of us was willing to look in the drawers of the refrigerator—but it was happily haphazard at least: We were busy, making some noise, turning the water in our buckets black, exerting ourselves to some end.

Around noon my mother produced a few crumpled twenties from some secret stash and stuffed them in my brother's hand. She instructed us to go to the store and buy groceries.

"Like what?" Gerard asked.

"Surprise me," she said.

So the two of us pushed a cart through the supermarket, like contestants on some idiotic game show, filling it more or less at random, with whatever caught our fancy, my brother inclined toward what was substantial and basic, bomb shelter foods, while I was tempted by what I thought of as delicacies—fancy cookies, weirdly shaped tropical fruit.

At home, we unloaded the groceries and my mother started cooking. She kept at it, more or less continuously as I recall, for a couple days, producing unlikely dishes at odd times, desserts before dawn, a midnight stew. It was nothing fancy; she was never an especially good cook, not very adventurous, too easily bored. Recipes, I suspect, struck her as too restrictive. She preferred seasoning a vat of something to her own peculiar taste. She favored the pungent and the unapologetic—liver and onions, sauerkraut, anything with garlic.

Gerard and I wandered into the kitchen from time to time, to check things out. We'd find my mother, covered with food stains and perspiring but happy, working a ball of dough with both hands, say, rolling and pounding it, forming it into no particular shape, like a kid with a big chunk of clay or a mud pie, absorbed in the sheer sensuous pleasure of it. On the table would be her latest creations: a couple of batches of chocolate chip cookies, which got progressively bigger and flatter as my mother ran out of patience and flour; a basket of gloriously greasy onion rings and for me, who didn't eat onions, great blobs of deep-fried batter; a cream of mushroom casserole covered with melted cheese. We'd snitch something and then duck out again.

At night, if the Twins were on the road, my mother and I would sometimes watch the game together in the living room on the portable black-and white television I carried up from the basement. It was a terrible set. The picture was dim, full of ghosts, shrunk slightly at the top and bottom so that all the players looked short and squat. On our TV, Harmon Killebrew, who was thick and compact to begin with, looked like a muscular troll. It worked as well as it did only because my mother made adjustments from time to time in the back with a butter knife, and when the picture started to flicker, she'd give the set a whack with a hairbrush, which, believe it or not, did the trick.

I was an antsy, nervous, semisuperstitious, thoroughly neurotic fan. In a tight spot late in the game, half believing that I could exert some control over the outcome, I'd sometimes leave the room, step into the bathroom and close the door or go outside and pace like an expectant father. I'd profess indifference ("so what if they tank now? who cares?"); I'd make dire predictions ("he's gonna chase a bad pitch and whiff, just watch"). I'd disown them, individually and collectively, swear them off like a bad habit. As if I could inoculate myself against disappointment.

My mother surprised me a little with her baseball savvy. As a girl, she used to play catch with her brother, and since he always got to use the one and only mitt, she developed a fine bare-handed technique—you pull back, cushion the blow and save your hands by giving with the ball. When I was nine or ten and still had aspirations to be a pitcher, she'd spent hours catching while I attempted to perfect my delivery. She used to sit in a lawn chair, a cigarette in her mouth, give me an open palm for a target—she refused a mitt—and would call out balls and strikes against an imaginary batter. Before she met my father, she claimed she dated a player for the old St. Paul Saints—the Dodgers' AAA affiliate in the '40s and '50s—a hard-throwing right-handed pitcher with a tendency to develop blisters on his throwing hand.

If the Twins committed some boner—walked the go-ahead run or threw to the wrong base, failed to get down a bunt or had a runner thrown out at third with nobody out—she let 'em have it, in no uncertain terms. What she hated above all else was excessive caution, short leads and intentional walks, pitchers who nibbled at the corners and any batter who took a called third strike.

"Take the bat off your shoulder," she'd mutter with a kind of contempt she ordinarily reserved for my father. "You can't hit if you don't swing."

We'd sit on the couch together, a bowl of popcorn between us, squinting into the snowy screen, talking mostly to ourselves and the players, only rarely to each other. I do remember we debated the merits of the sacrifice bunt. My mother had no use for it, but strategy aside, I liked the precision of the play, admired its neat execution. Besides, being a good bunter myself, I had a personal stake in thinking of it as a useful skill. I thought it was a good idea, sometimes.

"Look at it this way," she said. "You only get so many outs. Why give one away?"

While I loved the stars, Carew and Killebrew, Oliva and Chance, my mother pulled for her own unlikely favorites: Sandy Valdespino, who was famous for climbing the left-field fence to snatch back home-run balls; Rich Reese, Killebrew's caddie at first and our top pinch-hitter; Dave Boswell, who soaked his fingers in pickle brine to ward off the same kind of blisters that bedeviled her old flame with the Saints.

Home games I tuned in on my transistor. Herb Carneal, who was all business, did the play-by-play—he told you the pitch and location and provided a steady stream of facts about each player—with help from raucous old Halsey Hall, who was addicted to cheap cigars and full of shaggy stories about the old Minneapolis Millers and Nicollet Park, prone to fits of coughing laughter, best remembered perhaps for accidentally lighting his sport coat on fire during a broadcast.

A few times I parked the radio on the kitchen table while my mother and I played cards—gin, the only game she ever played. She smoked and drank Tab, purportedly a diet cola, with only one calorie, in tall bumpy bottles, horrible-tasting stuff that she didn't even bother to refrigerate. I'd tried it a couple of times, and it didn't taste like soda pop at all, not even bad soda pop; it was some other kind of beverage altogether, worse than medicinal: It was something you'd give to someone as a punishment or drink only on a dare. But my mother drank it, bottle after bottle, more or less continuously, coffee or Tab, always one or the other bitter drink at hand, sometimes both. She made me think of Denny McLain, the Detroit Tigers' bespectacled, organ-playing ace, who, it was said, knocked back more than a case of Pepsi a day.

My mother was a good cardplayer, a master of the maddeningly quick gin. She beat me game after game with a strategy I couldn't figure out and she refused to divulge. When I complained about my lousy cards, she clucked in mock sympathy. We played for a penny a point, and even though I never actually paid up, my mother kept meticulous track on the back of an envelope of what I theoretically owed her.

The Twins, who'd been trailing Chicago and Boston most of the season, always two, three games back, just sort of nipping at their heels, finally pulled even with the Red Sox after a memorable weekend series at the Met. On Saturday, Boswell beat Boston on a three-hitter. With the bases loaded and a one-run lead, he had had to face the great Elston Howard in his first at-bat since being traded from the Yankees. I was standing at the back door, half in and half out, full of dread but unable to turn away—it was like watching a game of Russian roulette—when Boswell struck him out.

And then on Sunday, George Walker showed up at the door with two tickets to the series finale. He held them up, almost apologetically. "I've got an extra," he said. "Are you interested?"

Was I interested. Dean Chance was pitching against Jim Lonborg, Boston's ace. "Go ahead," my mother said when I asked if I could go, uncharacteristically, almost suspiciously, agreeable. I got ready and headed down to Mr. Walker's as quickly as I could—before she had a chance to change her mind.

We had good seats on the first-base side. I'd been to plenty of games, but still felt something like wordless wonder in the face of the complex, vivid concreteness of the game that usually came to me so imperfectly, through Herb Carneal's words and the flickering, distorted images on our lousy television. It was like stepping inside your favorite book, like Dorothy landing in Oz. There was the impossible green of the grass and the bleached whiteness of the bases. The glistening baldness of Harmon Killebrew's head, uncovered during the national anthem, something you never saw on TV. George Scott's bulging biceps, Ted Uhlaender's chaw of tobacco the size of a tennis ball. The Twins-O-Gram in center field. The scurry of the grounds crew, the wail of vendors, the smell of mustard and cigar smoke.

Mr. Walker was a good man to watch a game with. He paid attention, kept careful score with his own ballpoint. He didn't talk too much. In the first inning, he bought us each a Saran Wrap–covered Coke and a bag of peanuts and then we focused on the field. Every once in a while he tapped me on the elbow and pointed out some strategic subtlety, some sideline shifting and signaling, some micro-maneuvering outside the ken of the Game of the Week's center-field camera. He showed me how Zoilo Versalles, the Twins' shortstop, who could glimpse the catcher's signs, would signal the outfielders, who would in turn cheat a couple of steps one way or

another depending on whether it was going to be a fastball or something off-speed. We watched Cesar Tovar
marking his lead off first base with a line in the dirt,
venturing a little farther and farther away from the base
each pitch until just when Mr. Walker called it—"this
time he's going"—he finally got a great jump and stole
second.

It had been overcast all day, and around the second
inning, some ominous-looking clouds started rolling in.
Chance, who was prone to wildness, worked fast, one
eye on the weather maybe, threw strikes and kept the
ball down. The Red Sox got only a couple of balls out
of the infield. It started to rain, just a drizzle at first,
then harder. Finally, in the top of the fourth inning,
with the score tied 0-0, the home plate ump signaled for
the groundskeepers to roll out the tarpaulin. The game
was delayed for twenty-five minutes. Mr. Walker and I
stayed put, under cover of the second deck's overhang.
We made some remarks about the game, but neither of
us mentioned the fact that Boston hadn't gotten a hit,
not even a base runner. We both knew it was bad luck
to talk about it.

After the rain let up, the groundskeepers uncovered
the infield and the pitchers warmed up again—Lonborg
not enough, according to Mr. Walker, who detected
something a little bit off in his mechanics. I nodded even
though I couldn't see what he was talking about. In any
case, the Twins got to him for a couple of runs in the
bottom of the fourth. Bob Allison doubled home Tovar
and then scored on a single by Rich Rollins.

Chance got the Sox out one, two, three in the top of the fifth. And then the rain really came, great sheets of it, a noisy deluge. "Two by two," someone in the crowd hollered. "Everybody onto the ark." Looking drowned and defeated, the grounds crew worked dutifully to cover the field, yanking ropes like doomed sailors in a hurricane, even though it was pretty clearly a lost cause—the field was already unplayable.

Bob Casey got on the PA after only twenty minutes or so and made the official announcement: the game had been called. It was, as we all knew, a legal game, a win for the Twins. Mr. Walker put his fingers in his mouth and whistled. Casey announced the official time of the game, just over an hour, and the attendance, 28,000, many of them already gone, and then declared, as he did after every game, with a phrase I'd always loved: "The totals on the board are correct." Dean Chance had pitched a rain-shortened, five-inning perfect game, fifteen up, fifteen down, a miniature masterpiece, an accomplishment as odd and as asterisked as you'll ever see.

The rain let up and we headed out to the parking lot, around the vast lakes of water, to Mr. Walker's car. I remembered prowling around the same lot earlier in the summer with my brother, but now walking along at George Walker's elbow, it seemed unreal, like a distant dream.

We drove home in contented silence, the post-game show on the radio giving us scores from around the league, both of us feeling, I imagined, that having witnessed something special, we'd somehow made history, too. When Mr. Walker pulled up in front of my house, I thanked him, and he gave me a thumbs-up.

I couldn't wait to tell my mother. "A perfect game," I said.

She was sitting at the kitchen table drinking coffee. "Semiperfect," she said. She'd listened to the game on the radio. "Partially perfect."

"Perfect is perfect," I said.

My mother lit a cigarette and grimacing a little, shifted in her chair. "And what's so great about perfect?"

My own summer baseball season ended sourly the following week when we got shut out in a play-off against a team from one of the northern suburbs. Before the game, during batting practice, I stood in right field supposedly shagging flies with Lou Chimera while Eddie Doyle, a dead right-handed pull hitter who had been in the cage for what seemed like forever, hit line drives to the left with a kind of machinelike consistency. Lou halfheartedly swatted at a bee with his mitt. "Watch out," he said. "JB's going to get you."

His mitt had been inscribed in black marker with the name John Boat, which Lou always claimed was the name not of a previous owner but of the glove itself. "Toss me John Boat," he would say. Or, more familiarly, "Has anybody seen Johnny?"

Usually, if you lingered too long in the cage, Mr. Walker would chase you, but now he was occupied elsewhere, working on the sidelines with the pitchers on their pick-off move. Doyle kept swinging. Lou cupped his hands and shouted toward home plate. "Take your time! Don't hurry on our account!" Doyle waved cheerfully at us and dug himself deeper into the box. He was our best hitter, but he didn't know when to quit.

When people say baseball is boring, I guess this is just what they're talking about—standing in the hot sun and waiting your turn, kicking dandelions, pounding your glove and spitting. But me, I never minded. I always sort of liked it, the slow-baked leisurely gab of it.

Lou and I had been talking about *Fear Strikes Out,* the old black-and-white movie biography of Jimmy Pearsall, the Boston Red Sox outfielder who suffered what is politely known as a nervous breakdown. He'd only recently retired after a long and modestly accomplished journeyman career. What he was famous for was eccentric behavior—doing sit-ups in center field, squirting home plate with a water pistol, running the bases backward. I used to study his baseball card image—he finished with the Angels—searching in vain for telltale signs of craziness. To me, he looked like a normal guy basically in his right mind.

Lou knew *Fear Strikes Out* practically by heart. When Mr. Walker wasn't around, he would sometimes climb the backstop, just like Tony Perkins in the movie, wild-eyed and shouting at an imaginary Karl Malden, the domineering father who drove him nuts. "Was I good enough? Was I good enough?" ("What do you think?" the rest of us would ask each other. "Nah.")

Today we were trying to think up possible titles for a sequel. *"Fear Grounds Out, Short to First,"* I said.

"Fear Flies Out Deep to Left," Lou said.

"Fear Gets Picked Off Second."

"Fear Draws an Intentional Walk."

"Fear Doubles into the Left-Field Corner."

"Fear Tries to Stretch a Double into a Triple and Gets Caught in a Rundown."

Finally, somebody shoehorned Doyle out of the cage and he came jogging out to join us.

"Greetings, ladies," he said. Ever so slowly, one finger at a time, he pulled off the black leather glove he wore when batting. It was a golf glove and, to my mind anyway, pure affectation.

"My dad says he saw you at the ballpark with Walker," he said to me. He was smiling, but it seemed forced, nervous and hostile, the way a man with knife smiles right before he robs you.

I felt busted. "Yeah?" I said.

"So what's the deal?" he said. "He gives you rides; he takes you to ballgames. Has George *adopted* you?"

I didn't know how to respond. I don't believe I'd ever heard an innocent word given an uglier spin.

Eddie's father was a lawyer and worked downtown. I knew he knew my father. Mr. Doyle had come up to me earlier in the season after a game and made much of shaking my hand. "Your dad," he said, and then, I believe he might have actually lapsed into the past tense, though it may simply have been his manner, which was pure funeral parlor, hushed and earnest. "Your father was a brilliant attorney. The best." He'd stood there, waiting for me to say something. It was horrible, all that knowing silence, the great suffocating weight of the unsaid, the sickening smell of his self-congratulatory tact. What could I say? I just put on my idea of solemn gratitude and nodded.

Eddie Doyle pulled a bag of sunflower seeds from the back pocket of his uniform pants and threw a handful into his mouth. "So is he like your father now?"

You're a lawyer, too, I thought, you relentless son of a bitch, just like your old man, just like mine. But before I had a chance to incriminate myself, Lou, God bless him, pointed to the empty batting cage and told me I better go in and take my hits.

In the top of the fifth, I was in the on-deck circle, swinging two bats, trying to time the delivery of the other team's pitcher, who was giving us fits. He was a tall lefty, all legs and elbows, with a spastic, jerky wind-up that had a little hitch, a kind of semicolon, right in the middle of it.

I sneaked a peak into the grandstand then, and that's when I spotted my father. He was standing on the top row of the bleachers behind home plate, wearing a suit and a raincoat, smoking a cigarette. He looked cool and impassive, not quite bored, more like his interest in the proceedings on the field was strictly professional. If he had been carrying a notebook, you might have thought he was a scout—a bird dog from one of the big league clubs in town to check out the local talent.

Marty Hauser grounded out feebly to the second

baseman, and I stepped into the batter's box. I looked at Mr. Walker down at third. There were two outs, the bases empty. He clapped his hands.

"Make some trouble," he hollered. "Light the fire."

But with this guy on the mound, I didn't feel like I was about to ignite much of anything. His teammates called him Robby, Robber, Robot, and there was definitely something mechanical, something not-quite-human about him. His motion was so jerky, so almost, but not quite right, it was spooky—like watching a pitcher throw under a strobe light. I couldn't pick up the ball properly, couldn't see where it was coming from.

The first pitch came in low and hard with a little hop in it, some weird southpaw English, and kicked up a cloud of dust in the catcher's mitt. Strike one. I took the second pitch—right across the knees again—for strike two.

I stepped out of the box and fiddled with my shoelaces. I heard my father's voice: "It only takes one, Sport. Show 'em what you're made of."

I stepped in and took a few practice swings, with as much confident menace as I could muster. What *was* I made of? I didn't have the least idea.

The pitch came in looking nice and fat, belt-high, but after I started to bring my hands forward, it broke, in and down, into the dirt, and too late to check my swing, I followed through stupidly, a great ill-timed whiff.

I turned and headed back to the dugout. Mr. Walker jogged past me.

"We'll get 'em next time," he said, but not, it seemed to me, with much conviction.

I tossed off my batting helmet and grabbed my mitt from the bench. When I took my position again at first base, I looked up into the stands again, trying to see my father, but it was too late—he was already gone.

On Labor Day, my mother tried her hand at what the cookbooks call holiday fare. She made a big batch of potato salad, laced too heavily with dill, but still impressive, a huge pan of it. She doctored up a casserole of baked beans with molasses and bacon; she even baked a chocolate cake. It was beautiful. Maybe that's why we ate hardly any of it. The dishes just sat on the table, like props in our domestic play.

That night we sat on the front steps, all of us, even my brother, which was unusual, eating watermelon, spitting seeds and listening to the second game of the Twins–Indians doubleheader. Having taken two out of three from the Tigers over the weekend, they had pulled ahead of the Red Sox into first place by a half a game.

Gerard produced some firecrackers, little ones, Zebras, I think, which he thought of as toys—the serious explosives left over from the Fourth, cherry bombs and M-80s, I knew, were stuffed in his sock drawer. My mother asked him for one. She lit it off her cigarette, held it long enough to make me nervous, staring at the burning fuse with the beginnings of a smile. Finally she tossed it off with a stiff, sweeping backhanded motion, peculiar but sort of stylish. She threw a few more, toward the curb, in hopes, I imagine, of getting a rise out of Mrs. Gunsher, the old biddy across the street. They weren't heavy-duty explosives, but they went off with a satisfactory crack, sharp and loud as gunfire.

"What do you think?" my mother said. "Not bad for a cripple."

The next day, coming up the front walk with a bag of groceries, she fell. I was right behind her and saw her ankle flop. She gasped and went down dead, like a half-back blindsided in the open field. The bag tore and a half-gallon milk carton burst.

She was okay, just a scrape on one hand, a three-corner tear in the knee of her slacks, more embarrassed than anything else. Lately I'd begun to notice how much labor it took for her just to do the simplest things—raise herself from the couch, walk down the hall into the kitchen, move from the sink to the refrigerator, to seat herself in a kitchen chair. Easy movements we take for granted, like getting in and out of a car, needed to be planned, calculated. She would check her right leg, as if it were not a part of her at all, locate it, adjust it, push and pull it, like a dog on a leash. Curbs were a challenge, I could tell, and most stairs she avoided altogether.

My mother pulled herself into a sitting position and waited there while I gathered up the groceries, staring at the frothy white puddle of milk on the sidewalk. It looked awfully weird in the light of day, almost beautiful, a big creamy oil spill.

"No use crying over it," I said.

My mother rarely out-and-out laughed, but I think she appreciated the joke. I held out my hand, and she pulled herself up. And then, with my mother holding so hard onto my arm it hurt, we made our way slowly over a slight incline where the sidewalk had buckled over the years, up the front steps, and into the house. When I walked with my mother, I noticed suddenly how full of obstacles the world was, how steep and cracked and slippery and full of holes it was, how dangerous.

It was only remission, after all. Every once in a while, I'd read a story in the paper about MS, always a new study. One suggested a link between the virus and certain childhood infections. Another described particular geographic areas—ours included—that were disproportionately affected. Still another study noted a high correlation between victims of the disease and dog owners. There was never a mention of a cure or breakthrough treatment. It wasn't hard to see through the so-called research—nobody really had much of an idea what the disease was all about or how to help the people who had it.

My mother's disease was going to return, with a vengeance. Pretty soon there would be no more singing, no more happy scrubbing. And all her cooking, much of it—maybe most of it—went to waste. It just sat in the refrigerator. I was still picky about food, wary of anything new. A lot of things I didn't eat because I just didn't like the looks of them. Gerard, surprisingly enough, big as he was, didn't eat that much, a couple of forkfuls here and there, a few cookies maybe, nothing off a plate. He might have put himself on a diet—I couldn't tell if he was losing weight or not but maybe he was. I rarely saw him eat anymore; he was consuming his calories elsewhere, in private, I guess.

My mother would take a bite or two and then lose interest. Finally she told me. We were sitting in the kitchen together late one night, my mother and I, eating sandwiches she'd fixed for us, grilled peanut butter for me, some kind of multistoried hero for herself. She had slathered on so much horseradish I was breathing it in from across the table. But so long as I wasn't the one eating it, I didn't really mind the smell. It was sort of bracing, like Mentholatum.

I was feeling pretty good. The Twins were in first place by two and a half games. The kitchen wasn't clean, but it was a run-of-the-mill mess, well within the range, not like before, nothing off the scale. It seemed to me then that I was a normal kid having a late snack with his normal mother. We'd been through a bad patch, sure, but things were getting better.

I told her my sandwich was good, which it was.

I noticed then that there were tears in her eyes. "What's the matter?" I said. I thought maybe she was sick, or choking on something. I stood up to help but she waved me off.

She admitted finally that everything tasted a little off to her, everything had a bitter, slightly metallic flavor. Try as she might, she couldn't do anything about it.

"Nothing tastes right," she said. "Nothing."

For her, food was a kind of cruel mirage, a mouth-watering promise full of sawdust.

She pushed her plate away and gave me a hard look, as if it were my fault. "It's only food," she said. "Right? Who cares?"

On the last weekend of the season, the Twins went into Boston, needing to win only one of the two games to clinch the pennant. We watched both games on our crappy portable, my mother chain-smoking and knocking back one Tab after another, me pacing and whining. Even my brother, who feigned indifference, stuck his head in the room every couple of innings to get the score.

Fenway Park was standing room only both days, full of dignitaries, including the vice president, Hubert Humphrey, whom we loved, even though he talked too much and supported the war, because he was from Minnesota, and a Democrat, who had shaken my mother's hand years ago at a fund-raiser and still sent our family a Christmas card every year with his and Muriel's signature stamped across the bottom.

On Saturday, with the Twins up one run in the third inning, Jim Kaat, our starting pitcher, hurt his elbow and had to leave the game. That's when I started to get a sinking feeling, when it occurred to me for the first time that the Twins might actually lose. Boston went ahead in the fifth, the Twins tied it up in the sixth, and then in the seventh, Carl Yastrzemski hit a three-run homer and put the game away. Harmon Killebrew hit a two-run shot in the ninth but it wasn't enough. The winning pitcher for Boston was Jose Santiago, a career relief pitcher who hadn't had a winning season since Albuquerque in 1960. He was just the sort of player my mother loved. We watched in silence as his teammates gleefully pummeled him with congratulations.

"Every dog has his day," my mother said.

"But why this dog?" I asked. "Why this day?"

On Sunday, Jim Lonborg pitched a seven-hitter, and with the Boston fans going crazy—they booed Killebrew for goodness sake, the nicest guy in the world—Yastrzemski got four straight hits, and the Red Sox won five to three. Rich Rollins hit a soft pop-up to the shortstop for the last out, and my mother leaned forward and jammed the television off with her cane. The screen went dark, and just like that, our season was over.

CHAPTER TEN

Our caseworker's name was Alice Quigley. She had beautiful blonde hair that smelled sweet, like peaches. (My college girlfriend's hair smelled the same way, and I sometimes wondered whether it was a fragrance—a certain brand of shampoo—that I fell for.) She must have been in her early twenties, a newly minted master of social work, I suppose, full of earnest idealism.

In September, she had stopped by in order to get acquainted. She had a handful of paperwork, things for my mother to sign. She'd brought literature about the state chapter of the multiple sclerosis society, too, information about support groups and a hot-line, a copy of their glossy monthly magazine.

"No thanks," my mother said. She wasn't interested in discounted wheelchair rentals; she didn't want to hear about other people's problems.

Alice Quigley nodded a lot and took some notes. I sat next to her on our swayback sofa, close enough to breathe her essence, to admire the elegance of her crossed ankles. On the way out, she shook my hand and said she was pleased to meet me. She asked me a few questions about my schoolwork, like the small talk of a nurse preparing an inoculation, and I said whatever I thought would please her. She called me by my real given name, which no one else did, except in derision, but when she spoke it, it didn't sound ridiculous. It was clear to me that she was a good person. Maybe that's why we tormented her.

Saturdays in October I did yardwork at Mr. Walker's house and talked to him, mostly about baseball, about the World Series. I'd been rooting for the Red Sox, because according to my fan's convoluted logic, a win for them, who'd beaten my team, would reflect well on the Twins—and me, too, of course—and place us in their reflected world-championship glory, just one game away from taking it all ourselves. Besides, I felt loyal to the A.L.—to me, the National League would always be a foreign country. But Lonborg and Yastrzemski proved they were only human after all, and St. Louis beat them in seven games.

"Gibson is awesome," I said.

I admired his fierceness, that stare. His fastball, Mr. Walker told me, came in low, spinning so tight and hard, it would be rising as it crossed the plate. No wonder he terrified people.

We were taking a break, sipping Cokes on the back steps surrounded by tools. We'd spent most of the afternoon getting his flower beds ready for the long winter, which, on this golden day, seemed unimaginably far off.

But Minnesota was brutal on rose bushes, though Mr. Walker claimed if you did it right—cut them back short, covered them with hay, then plastic—they'd survive in even the worst weather. The year before, he told me, when the temperature had never climbed above zero for one whole week in January, he hadn't lost a single plant.

Mr. Walker asked me how school was going, how I liked eighth grade.

"Fine," I said.

It's not the sort of thing you broadcast, but I'd always liked school, especially since my mother got sick, welcomed the start of the new year, everything fresh and new—fresh notebooks, freshly waxed floors, new teachers—a fresh batch of relatively kindly adults. Hell, I even liked quizzes and tests, regular opportunities to succeed, to feel like I was good at something. I enjoyed the sense of accomplishment, the illusion of progress.

"What's your favorite subject?" Mr. Walker asked.

I had to think about it. "Social studies," I told him. I liked Mr. Baumgarten, his flowered ties and his jokes. He'd recently prohibited me from pulling any more Current Events from the sports page, but I didn't mind.

Mr. Walker wondered how things were going at home. "How is your mother feeling?"

I took a long stinging slug of my Coke. It was my style to be cautious in my evasions, preferring partial truth to the out-and-out lie.

"She's up and around," I said.

George Walker wasn't stupid. He'd seen her. He

knew what he knew. But he just nodded and waited for me to say more.

There were lots of things I could have told him. I didn't tell him that Mrs. Arvin at the dairy store hollered at me about a bad check my mother had written, and then stuck her hand out, expecting me to make it good. I didn't tell him that I had found two joints in my brother's dresser drawer and was worried about what else he might be trying. I didn't tell him that to make some room in the kitchen, my mother had stuffed a mess of dishes—dirty still, covered with crumbs, smeared with ketchup—into cardboard cartons and piled them in the back porch. I didn't tell him that I had nightmares about my father and couldn't sleep without a light on.

And I didn't tell him that a social worker had been to our house that morning. My mother had covered the front door window with opaque contact paper, but there was a loose corner, so you could peek out. I'd heard a knock and taken a look. I could see Alice Quigley's red Volkswagen parked at the curb. I could see the golden sheen of the top of her head, a black velvet band, like a headset, holding her hair in place. I wanted to open the door and invite her in. Maybe she remembered my name. I wouldn't have minded hearing her say it again. But I knew the rules. Most of the time, we didn't open the door, not for her, not for anyone. Just on general principle. People who came to the front door all wanted something. So I just stood there, waiting, just inches away from her, my heart pounding, until she turned and walked away. I'd wanted to shout and wave my arms and call her back. Right then, I felt crazed and hopeless. How would I explain that to Mr. Walker?

I picked up his pruner from the step and gripped it, clipping idly at nothing. I liked the feel of it, its weight and power. The thing was shiny and heavy and murderously effective—it sliced branches an inch in diameter like cooked carrots; it would cut through bone, I imagined, take off a finger like nothing.

"Do you think I could borrow this?" I asked.

"I don't see why not," he said.

"Just for a little while," I said. "Just long enough to clean up our yard a little bit."

Mr. Walker seemed pleased. "Yes," he said. "That's a great idea."

He asked me if I wanted some help.

I thought about it. My mother looking out the kitchen window and spotting me and Mr. Walker back there, knee-deep in weeds, cutting and pruning, like a couple of GIs hacking their way through the jungle—an invasion. She called him Mr. Fixit, or else *Coach,* which she pronounced in mocking italics.

"No," I said. "I don't think so. Not this time."

"All right," he said. "Not this time."

But he did his best to get me ready—armed and equipped me, outfitted and instructed me, like a seasoned guide sending a novice into the wilderness for the first time. Shears and a long-handled scythe, smooth and sleek as a Louisville Slugger. A pair of gloves. A bushel basket and a box of lawn bags.

The next morning I spread out Mr. Walker's things and went to work. I pulled weeds—some flowers, too, I'm afraid, I couldn't really tell the difference—in front of our house, cut back our hedge, and raked a big pile of marble-hard crab apples that had fallen from our tree in front. To make much of a real difference, of course, I'd have had to apply myself with a steadiness of purpose that seemed beyond me. This was a spasm, not a program. I had good intentions but not much staying power. But at least for just the moment I felt as though like I was doing something. My eyes were stinging with sweat. If Alice Quigley pulled up right then in her little red Bug, I imagined, she would be impressed. She would see what kind of kid I really was.

Alice Quigley made her last home visit in November. Because we didn't have a telephone, it must have been difficult for her to stay in touch. Finally, she sent us a neatly printed postcard suggesting a date later in the month—Saturday afternoon at three.

It seemed far off, but the day finally arrived, gray and bitter cold. I did some half-assed housecleaning by way of preparation. I filled a grocery bag with pop cans and emptied my mother's ash trays. I stashed dirty clothes in the front closet. I pushed the worst furniture—two wobbly, half-broken dining room chairs and a worn recliner, leaking its stuffing—into a corner and straightened the couch cover so she would have a decent place to sit.

My mother just watched. "Should I be polishing the crystal?" she asked.

She refused to take any of it seriously—social workers, home visits, Alice Quigley. Somehow she maintained a completely unjustified, nearly insane belief in our specialness, in the distance between our family and everyone else in the files. She read the pathetic stories in the newspaper at Christmas, about needy families with no trees, and felt sorry for them. They didn't apply to us. We were better and smarter, she believed, just passing through, suffering only a few bad breaks and temporary setbacks. That we needed help, that this sweet little girl could give it to us, seemed to strike her as absurd. Or maybe just too humiliating even to acknowledge.

After lunch, my brother and I built a fire in the living room. We hadn't used the fireplace in years, but we got the flue open and swept out three or four inches of ashy debris from the bottom. Gerard put a match to some crumpled newspapers and I fed in a few cardboard boxes and pieces of scrap lumber I found in the garage. We kept the fire going all afternoon, idly, out of sheer boredom. Alice might enjoy it, I imagined. When the doorbell rang, we were sitting on the floor watching the orange flames flicker, hot-faced, half-hypnotized.

My mother opened the door with a big smile.

"Alice," she said. "Welcome to Welfareland."

Alice Quigley was holding a stack of file folders and a black appointment book with colored tabs. She took off her coat and shook hands all around. She sat on the couch and smoothed her skirt. She was wearing dark tights and heavy black shoes, like a farmer's wife. I sat cross-legged on the floor facing the couch, close enough to inhale her scent.

"Well," she said. She shuffled her papers. "How is everything?"

"Dandy," my mother said. She was perched on the corner of the coffee table, her hands resting on the handle of cane. "Couldn't be better," she said.

Gerard poked the fire and made a rude noise, barely audible.

I wished Alice Quigley would just take charge, tell my mother to cut the crap and shape up. Or just take me away. For weeks I had been imagining scenarios of unlikely rescue. That she would, say, bring me to her place and treat me like a lost kid at the police station, give me all the ice cream I could eat. I pictured the two of us together in her apartment, where I just knew she kept cats, sitting side by side on the couch, chatting happily like old friends. Maybe she would help me with my homework. The more I thought about her, the easier it was to imagine that she took a special interest in me, that we had some kind of unspoken understanding and intimacy.

In reality, Alice Quigley was too flustered to pay much attention to me. She meant well, no doubt, but she was in over her head.

"What a lovely skirt," my mother said.

"Thank you," Alice said.

"The roof is leaking," my mother said. "The water heater is shot."

Alice held a piece of paper on her lap and tried to

make a note, but couldn't get her ballpoint to write. My mother lit up a cigarette and started to say something, but was overcome by a fit of coughing.

"I'll see what I can do," Alice said.

She was too polite to stare, but I could see her stealing glances around the house, and I felt newly ashamed. The walls were still only partially painted, for one thing, one third lemon yellow, the rest dingy beige. There were wispy bundles of dog hair gathered in the corners, food stains on the arm of the couch. The room was nothing but dust and crooked lampshades.

Our fire, meanwhile, was dying. And then, in a moment of what must have been sudden inspiration, my brother stood and walked to where I had shoved the broken furniture. He put his foot on the padded seat of one of the dining room chairs and pulled off a front leg. He took it over to the fireplace and pitched it in. The varnish crinkled and smoked. Nobody said anything. We just stared. Eventually it caught fire. Lying on the grate with the flames lapping it, that chair leg—it was hardwood, cherry, I think—looked gruesome, like a human limb.

Alice Quigley started to ask a question, something about my father, and just left it hanging. She was rattled. "Has Mr. Hawkins . . ."

"No," my mother said. She could keep a straight face. Still, she was delighted, I could just tell.

Gerard threw in the other leg, and then pried the back off and tossed that in too. The padding sparked and smoldered and then flared into flame. I felt sick to my stomach.

Alice was fluttering on the couch now, gathering up her papers, getting ready to bolt.

I stood up. "Excuse me," I said. "Would you like something to drink?"

I could hear Gerard snort. "Something to drink?" she said.

"A Coke?" I said. "Some tea?"

"Tea would be nice," she said. "Thank you."

In the kitchen, I heated some water and found a bag of Lipton's in the cupboard. I rinsed one of my mother's coffee cups. Gerard came in and watched while I filled the cup and dropped in the tea bag. I looped the string around the cup's handle as I had seen it done somewhere. In the other room, I could hear my mother coughing, a deep, tubercular liquid rattling.

I squeezed in a few drops of juice from a plastic lemon that had been rolling around our refrigerator for as long as I could remember and put the cup on a small plate, which was the closest thing to a saucer I could find.

"Wait," my brother said. He opened a cupboard door and brought down a little bottle of Tabasco. He shook in one orange drop, then another, and another.

"There," he said. He set the hot sauce on the counter.

"Now that's more like it," he said. He looked at me, waiting to see what I would do.

I believed then that nothing was going to change. Alice Quigley was going to get into her red VW Bug and drive off. She would file a report, make a mark next to our name in her little book. That was it.

"Cute," I said.

"Exactly," he said. "Just like little Miss Alice."

By the time I got the cup washed and found another tea bag, Alice Quigley was already headed out the door. She saw me holding the cup and saucer and smiled. She thanked me by name. "I need to take a rain check on the tea," she said. "Next time."

She told my mother that I was eligible for a Big Brother and that she was certain she could get one lined up in a matter of weeks. I'd seen the public service spots on television. They took you to ballgames, bought you pizza.

"He's got a big brother," my mother said. "One is enough."

"Give it some thought," Alice said. "I'll be in touch."

My mother just shrugged her shoulders.

We stood in the doorway, the three of us, and watched her walk to her car.

"Jeez," Gerard said. "What's her problem?"

Afterward, I discovered that she'd left her appointment book on the couch. I put it aside for her, thinking she'd come back for it, but she never did. That was our last home visit.

CHAPTER ELEVEN

After that, we spent more and more time in the car, going nowhere in particular, still just cruising, stopping only for gas and fast food, burgers and fries and shakes, which we ate on the fly. As far as we knew anyway, my father had not returned since that first night we beat him out the door. But still, who wants to sit around waiting? It felt good to be on the move. It was nothing we planned or even talked about. We'd be at home in the evening, sitting around, doing nothing, like barracked soldiers, bored and scared, the television playing and nobody watching; then, my mother would pick up her car keys.

Sometimes Gerard came along, sometimes not. He'd gotten a job working after school and weekends at a local pharmacy—he had to wear a clip-on bow tie, which he hated, but the money was good. He retailed rubbers to his classmates and liked to brag about the exorbitant rates some stupid Larrys would pay the night of a mixer. In our house, he came and went irregularly and unpredictably, a big angry ghost. In the middle of the night, half asleep, I'd dimly become aware of his presence in our room: see his big shadow in the door-way and the orange glow of a cigarette, hear his keys and change jangling, the thud of his big shoes on the floor. When he did come along in the car, it was with an attitude, like he was slumming, taking a spin on a kiddie ride. Me, I loved those improvisational jaunts.

My mother found out where my father was living, and we spent a lot of time casing his place, a second-story apartment in a brick building on Grand Avenue. We'd drive by it again and again, making different approaches, idling in the alley out back, peering up at his window, hoping to see—what? I don't know. Looking for some-thing incriminating, I guess, trying to catch him in the act, any act.

My mother liked to provide a little running commen-tary, talked to my father while she was inspecting his place, the way someone might talk to the fish they're trying to catch—disconnected bits of half-nonsense, sweet ruthless nothings.

"What have we here?" she'd say to a shadow in his room. "Getting ready for a night on the town?"

She was fascinated by even a glimpse of his things—curtains, a lamp, a picture on the wall—driven, I guess, by some kind of angry curiosity, a desire to doc-ument how he was spending the money we had a claim on, to measure the distance between us, his extravagance and our squalor. His apartment had dark woodwork and some kind of chandelier. In our house, my mother had recently taken to patching things with ninety-nine-cents-a-roll, self-adhesive contact paper—fleurs-de-lis on the splintered door panels my father had kicked out, wood-grain on the scarred kitchen cupboards. She joked about how tacky it was, but with or without irony, it was still tacky.

"Sweet dreams," she said, when the lights went out. "May you die in your sleep."

Once, at my mother's urging, I dashed into the lobby and looked around. I was too scared to notice much, but it felt dim and illicit in there—dark carpeting, heavy woodwork and stained glass, a whiff of cologne and whiskey in the air, the aroma of adult pleasure. There were six metal boxes with last names printed on little labels, except for one, which I assume was his. I rifled through the stuff in the mail bin—all of it junk, just catalogs and solicitations—and beat it back to the car.

Sometimes I'd do homework, right in the car. Assignments came at me as regular and as insistent as bills, and I wanted to keep my head above water—tackle it the way Mr. Walker and I did yardwork, step-by-step. At least I could keep my school accounts in the black. So while my mother drove, I'd flick on the overhead light and read and underline in my English anthology or my science text. Balance a notebook on my knee and scratch out my math problems. It made things more interesting to be on the move. I'd be reading something—an Edgar Allen Poe story, a chapter on ocean life—or working an equation, and I'd look up and find myself someplace I'd never been before: in the shadows of the old round tower at Fort Snelling, circling some perfect little lake, looking up at the broken windows of a spooky abandoned warehouse.

At some point I started telling my brother and mother stories about the people we'd see, mundane little histories at first—he's a big-shot doctor headed for surgery, she's got a hot date. Whatever came into my head. We were bored, that's all, and it was better than playing license plate bingo. My mother and Gerard seemed to enjoy it. If we'd see something even vaguely remarkable—a guy driving a pickup loaded with pinball machines, a bus stop bench full of old ladies all dolled up, a station wagon containing two nuns and a Great Dane—and I didn't offer something, they'd start asking me questions. "Where's he going? What are *they* up to?" I liked that expectant pause, the space waiting to be filled. I liked them listening to me.

After a while, my stories became gradually more mysterious—shadowy characters with darker motives on more complex journeys—and finally, criminal. I must have felt as if I needed to keep upping the ante. My head was full of TV cop shows, the Hardy Boys, stuff like that. It came surprisingly easy to me—kidnappings, hostages, desperately scrawled pleas for help pressed against the glass.

"See that guy in the Caddie?" I said. He was stopped next to us at a light on University Avenue. It was a Monday night, eleven o'clock, maybe midnight.

"Yeah?" Gerard said. He acted like a tough guy, but he was really interested. Even my mother took a look.

"He's the wheelman for a mobster," I said. "He's got a body in the trunk."

And—this is the strange part, the scary part really—as soon as I said it, this guy, just a fat-faced guy with slicked-back hair gripping the wheel with black gloves, took on the coloring of menace. Right before my eyes, he *became* a dangerous character. Didn't matter that I'd made him up, I was still a little afraid of him.

"A body?" Gerard said. "Holy shit."

"Sawed up into little pieces," I said. "Wrapped in butcher paper."

Somehow *we* became part of this story. I think it might have been my mother's idea to follow him. Or if I suggested it, she at least played along. I wouldn't have had to ask her twice. He headed down University into downtown St. Paul, and we tailed him.

"Not so close, Ma," Gerard said. "Hang back a little. Keep your distance."

The man pulled up to a drive-by box in front of the post office. He put his flashers on, leaned across the front seat, and tossed something in.

"He's mailing a piece of the body to his next target," I said. "Sending a message. That's how these guys operate."

"What piece?" Gerard said.

"Don't ask," I said.

The man pulled away then, and we stayed with him, north past the capitol and down Larpenteur or Payne into the East Side, Frogtown, which was pretty much unknown to us—block after block of corner bars and hardware stores. We lost him at one light but caught up to him at the next.

"He's on to us," Gerard said, and sure enough, we could see him checking the rearview mirror.

"Maybe we should ease off," I said. "A little." I was afraid there might be trouble.

The Cadillac made three consecutive right turns on dark side streets, and so did we. "Okay, Ma," Gerard said. "Enough is enough."

But I could tell there was no way was she going to give it up now. She was in it for the duration, I was afraid. She liked a little dangerous fun.

He rolled through a four-way stop, then, and so did my mother. He speeded up, and she stayed right with him. Finally, the Caddie pulled over. It was in the middle of a block of doubles, right under a street lamp. My mother slowed way down, almost to a stop.

Under the lights we got a good look at him. He didn't look like a killer now; he looked like my Uncle Florian. He was white-eyed and sweaty, stubbing out a butt in beanbag ashtray on the dash, craning his neck over his shoulder and squinting in our direction. He was guilty of something, I suppose—who isn't?—and maybe he figured this was his moment of reckoning. He was scared of *us*.

My mother hit him with the high beams.

"For crying out loud," Gerard said.

She pulled around him and gunned it then, and we

left him there, the poor bastard, trying to find the words, maybe, he would use to explain to someone what it was exactly that had just happened to him.

We begged my mother to let us stay home from school the next day. Nothing doing. I overslept and arrived late, no homework, no lunch, my clothes wrinkled, just in time to get creamed on Mr. Baumgarten's social studies exam. I could barely keep my eyes open, much less recall the particulars of the Magna Carta. "Whatcha get?" Patty Potter wanted to know, and I told her. My only rival in the class when it came to good grades, she couldn't believe it. "Twelve wrong?" she said and wrinkled her little nose.

To hell with you, I thought, your perfect papers, your gold-star life.

"You drive," my mother said, and handed me the keys. We were in the parking lot of Kroger's on Robert Street. It was Sunday morning, seven-thirty, maybe eight o'clock. My mother and I, both of us early risers, had been in the store buying bread and milk while Gerard slept in. It was just us and the stock boys, one sleepy girl at the checkout.

"Me?" I said.

"Sure," she said. "Why not?"

"I'm too young," I said.

"You're never too young to learn," she said.

My brother seemed like a much more likely candidate than me for a driving lesson, if that's what this was. He was old enough for a learner's permit and was scheduled to take driver's ed at school next term. He talked about cars and driving all the time. "When I get my license," he would say again and again, and then fill in the blank with some unrelated, unlikely future-tense fantasy or resolution. "When I get my license," he'd say, and then sometimes trail off, enjoying just the sound of it, I guess.

I slid across into the driver's seat and grabbed the wheel.

"What now?" I said.

The car had an automatic transmission at least, but still, I wasn't sure what to do. Of course, I'd been watching my mother drive, but she wasn't the best model. She drove with her left foot, for one thing, but besides that, she was impatient and volatile behind the wheel, hardly an exemplary driver. She cut through gas stations rather than wait for red lights, she tailgated, she passed on the right. She cursed old people and school buses.

"Put it in drive," my mother said. George Walker taught driver's education at the high school. I was certain that his behind-the-wheel instruction was not nearly so casual; he'd have some kind of checklist of techniques to master, a sensible series of commands to follow.

My mother watched me tug for a while on the shift. "Pull it toward you," she said. I did and eventually—after overshooting the "D" coming and going—put the car in gear.

"Good," she said. "Now you're driving."

I held tight onto the wheel as the car slowly rolled

forward. I felt like I was riding something, some half-wild living thing, a big rumbling beast. The car inched forward across the lot, which was huge and now, at this hour, practically empty. There were some potholes and a couple of light standards, not much potential to do any serious damage. I felt a little scared, but I liked it, too, all that motorized weight, like a tank, rolling forward with me—theoretically at least—in control.

We were pointing toward the middle of the empty lot, a little boat headed out to sea.

"Give it some gas, for crying out loud," my mother said.

I located the accelerator—my mother always called it the exhilarator—and punched it, hard, and the car lurched forward with a squeal.

"That's more like it," she said.

With a little practice, I figured out how to moderate the gas pedal. I got the hang of steering. We circumnavigated the lot a few times in easy ten-mile-an-hour loops. I kept my distance from the light poles and the other parked cars. It was easier than I had imagined. My mother sat leaning on the door, staring vaguely out the window and smoking a Pall Mall, not looking the least bit nervous or scared. If anything, she looked bored.

I watched the numbers spin slowly on the odometer, four-tenths of a mile around the lot, so that even though we weren't really going anywhere, I still felt important and purposeful—that's the joy of motion. But after a while, I noticed that traffic was starting to pick up on Robert Street and a couple more cars had turned into the lot.

"What about the brake?" I asked.

"Don't worry about the brake," my mother said. "The brake's not that important."

A few days later, we were in the car, my mother driving, me in the front seat beside her, both of us slurping monster malts from Dairy Queen, debating whether or not it made any sense to call her favorite flavor a *hot* fudge malt, when right in the middle of the Grand hill, halfway up, my mother suddenly cut a screaming U-turn and headed back down. It threw me against the side of the car and sent a shower of stuff flying off the dashboard—coffee cups, a tennis ball, ketchup packets.

"What the hell," I said.

Suddenly we were in hot pursuit, of something, my mother didn't say what, but I had a pretty good idea. She was hunched over the wheel, watching the road intently, edging the car into the other lane in order to get a better look at something.

We stopped for a red light at the bottom of the hill, and then, across the intersection, turned into a Stop-and-Go, a combination gas station and liquor store, open all night, a place my mother claimed got held up every couple of weeks. She circled the pumps and then backed into a spot next to a Dumpster. It was a tiny place, just a brightly lit hut with an ice cooler and cases of motor oil stacked out front. Inside we could see a cashier perched on a tall stool.

When my father stepped out of the store, we could see him plain as day.

"Why don't you tell me about that guy?" my mother said. "What's his story?"

Wearing a long camel hair overcoat, a paper bag under his arm, tapping a pack of cigarettes. I didn't know what to say. He looked dapper and dangerous, perfumed and ruthless, like a movie crime boss.

We watched him walk across the lot and get into a big beige boat of a car with a vinyl roof.

"It's none other than Harlan Hawkins Senior," my mother said, "aka The Hawk. Famous attorney and deadbeat. Looks like he's making a rare appearance at a liquor store."

"Imagine that," I said.

"If I had a gun," my mother said, "I'd shoot him."

It felt strange watching him like that, without his knowing it, as if we really were assassins or something.

My father took a long time starting his car, but finally, after a certain amount of shadowy adjustment inside—he seemed to be fiddling with the vents or the radio, lighting a cigarette—the lights came on and he pulled out.

We followed him down West Seventh, away from downtown, but when a slow-moving panel truck cut in front of us, we missed the light on St. Clair, and lost him.

"Son of a bitch," my mother said.

"Big deal," I said. "He got away."

I felt relieved. I had no idea what she had in mind, and I didn't really want to find out.

"We'll see about that," my mother said.

She kept driving and another mile or so down Seventh, I spotted his car on a dark side street, parked a generous distance from the curb. He didn't park cars, my mother used to say, he dropped them, abandoned them, and walked away. We pulled in right behind.

It was hard to tell where my father might have gone. The street was lined with big Victorians, and the one he'd parked in front of had the porch light on. Right around the corner on Seventh Street, there was a bar, a Laundromat, a barbershop, and a massage parlor.

My mother cut the engine and lit a cigarette. We sat there in silence together, maintaining an unlikely stakeout, for what felt like an awfully long time. But my mother didn't seem to be in any hurry. She smoked one cigarette after another, her eyes fixed on my father's car, totally absorbed, watching a movie that only she could see.

It didn't make a lot of sense. When the divorce became final, my mother had posted the decree on the refrigerator door with a magnet, like an A paper. Now, if we passed a wedding party, a car tied with tin cans just pulling away from the church, say, the happy couple smooching in the backseat, she would honk and yell, "Suckers." When my father came back to the house, we split. I'd assumed that was the whole point of having a car—to get away from him. But now we were trailing him. If it ever was, it wasn't funny anymore.

"What are we waiting for?" I asked.

It was hard to imagine what my mother wanted with him. Deep down, I guess, she wanted either to kill him or remarry him—probably both.

A woman in a parka and wrapped in a long red scarf came down the sidewalk. She was holding two huskies on leashes, one in each hand. The dogs stopped to sniff a tree next to our car, and she yanked them forward. Suddenly, for the first time in a long time, I missed our dog, Heston, who was squirrelly and nipped people and ran away, but never tired of playing with me. I wished I was home, in the backyard, throwing the tennis ball for him.

"Come on," I said. "I gotta go to the bathroom."

"Okay," she said at last. "Okay. Give me something to write with."

I rifled the glove compartment and finally, after some blind reaching, brought up something from beneath the seat and handed it over to my mother.

She scribbled a note. Magic marker on a paper napkin, a few bold strokes. I have no idea what it said. But I do know this. It was short and sweet, probably pungent. If it was a full sentence, I suspect it was an imperative. I don't suppose she felt the need to sign it.

"I'll be right back," she said.

She opened her door and, pushing off with a grunt and a grimace, got out from behind the wheel. She walked slowly, dragging her bad foot, her hand on the hood of our car, not really leaning on it for support exactly, more like she was just maintaining contact, like a blind person. It was how she used her cane, or the grocery cart or my arm or the kitchen counter at home—to stay grounded. She moved around to the front of my father's car.

I didn't know what she was doing. She tucked the napkin note under the car's windshield, like a parking ticket, and then walked slowly along the car on the

curbside, with her hand extended, as if she were drawing a line on the car with a pen.

I rolled my window down and could hear a kind of
pained metallic squeak. There were no sparks but it had
that sound.

"Sweet Jesus," I said. She was keying his car.

My mother was standing at the passenger side, holding on to the door handle with one hand for balance,
digging with her other into the door. She inched her
way toward the back of the car and went to work on the
rear quarter panel. It seemed to be taking an awfully
long time for her to get the job done.

"Hurry up," I said. Part of me wanted to get out and
help, to do something besides watch.

A car turned off Seventh and fixed her for a moment
in its headlights, but she didn't flinch. She was standing
at the back of the car now, her hand moving in stiff circles, her mouth tight with concentration, etching a few
decorative swirls on the trunk, a little icing on the cake.

I stuck my head out the window and shouted.
"Knock it off. You're gonna get us arrested."

She looked up, looking a little surprised, as if she'd
forgotten I was there, and gave me a little beauty-queen
wave with her free hand.

Afterward, back in the car, parked in the Mr. Donut
lot and passing a box of day-old doughnut holes back
and forth, she seemed offended when I suggested she'd
done something wrong.

"Vandalism?" she said. "Vandalism?"

"Vandalism," I said.

"That's strong language," my mother said. "That's a serious charge to fling at someone."

"What do you call it then?" I asked.

She licked powdered sugar from her upper lip and gave it some thought. I knew she was going to come up with something good. "An act of righteous indignation," she said.

"Righteous what?" I said. I liked the sound of it and wanted to hear her say it again.

"Indignation," she said.

"That's a crock," I said, trying my best not to smile. "Tell it to the judge."

CHAPTER TWELVE

A few days after Christmas my father coughed up a big chunk of money. Sent it over—a long yellow check for two grand—tucked inside a cellophane-wrapped basket of fruit. A cabby brought it to the house close to midnight. We almost didn't open the door. I had become a hair-trigger light sleeper—like a dog, eyes closed but still alert, ready to scramble to my feet—roused in an instant by the sound of an engine out front. I looked out my bedroom window and saw the cab idling at the curb with its flashers on.

When I came down the stairs, my mother was standing at the front door, cane in hand, peeking through the window.

"It's a cab," I said.

She opened the door slowly, raised her cane, and half pointed it at the poor guy, not brandishing it exactly, but still. Any monkey business, she was going to let him have it, three prongs to the groin.

"No charge," he said, and handed it over. "From Mr. Hawkins."

. . .

We sat at the kitchen table then, the basket in front of us, and my mother passed the check around, a little late-night show-and-tell. The fruit was huge, grotesquely out of proportion, apples, oranges, pink and yellow grape-fruit, great globes of waxen, artificial-looking, too-vivid perfection. My brother scooped up a handful of nuts that were sprinkled in the bottom along with some foil-wrapped candies.

"It's no good," he said.

"What do you mean?" I said.

It looked fine to me. First National Bank. The amount of two thousand dollars and no one hundreds. My father's flamboyant signature at the bottom.

"It's gonna bounce," Gerard said.

My mother picked up a red Delicious and took a big crackling bite.

"Gimme that," she said. I slid the check across the table, and she studied it at arm's length, thoughtfully chewing her apple.

"He won the tractor case," she said finally. "That's what happened."

We'd been hearing about it for years, my father's tractor case. A teenage boy got his overalls tangled up in the power shaft of his neighbor's International Har-vester, both legs chewed up, a double amputation. My father went after the farmer, who had removed the guard—they all did for some reason—and the manufac-turer, too.

"I can just see him," my mother said. "Sobbing into

his hankie for the poor farm boy. Making the case for pain and suffering."

Juries loved my father apparently, and he knew it. When they were first married, my mother told me, he used to perform his summations for her. She said he could cry on cue.

"This unfortunate youth," Gerard said, his voice thick with counterfeit emotion, a fat finger raised and wagging in the air, weirdly out of synch with his words. "Cut down in the prime of life."

"Laid low in the bloom of youth," I said.

My brother was good—he had those crazy gestures down cold—and I was hoping that if I fed him some lines, he would keep it up. But he'd already run out of gas, resumed his normal demeanor, and started picking through the bottom of the fruit basket for more nuts.

"What about us?" he said. "What about *our* pain and suffering?"

My mother snorted.

"Two thousand bucks," I said. "It's nothing to sneeze at."

"Too little," Gerard said. "Too late."

"It's a bone," my mother said. "That's what it is. He's throwing us a bone."

"Cheap bastard," Gerard said.

"What do you mean, a bone?" I said.

"Look," my mother said. "Remember child support? Remember alimony? He thinks that if he tosses off one check and a bunch of oranges—playing the big shot, same as always—we'll just go gaga with gratitude. And then he's off the hook."

"Maybe this is just the first," I said. "Maybe he's going to start sending checks every month."

"Maybe," my brother said, a big fake smile on his fat face, nodding, his eyes wide with dumb, doglike trust. "Maybe."

When he spoke it like that, I understood, what a foolish word it was.

"So what do we do with this?" I asked.

My mother gave me a look, sad exasperation, as if to say, haven't I taught you anything? You've got a lot to learn.

"Cash it," she said.

Through a shrewd combination of promises, pleas, and strategic partial payments, my mother had for many months kept us from utter ruin. We were clothed, fed, and housed. On our measly county check, it couldn't have been easy. But she was good, a deft spinner of financial plates. She used cash only when absolutely necessary. Checks offered more creative possibilities. She postdated checks, kited checks, and always wrote them for more than the amount due—five dollars over, ten dollars over, whatever they'd allow. Even if it bounced, she had some cash in hand. We just stayed out of the stores where her name was on the list. She borrowed from Peter to pay Paul back just enough to borrow some more from Paul. She knew just how much she had to send Northern States Power to keep our shit turned on.

At Christmas, somehow, there'd even been gifts. Gerard had wrapped up a carton of Pall Malls for my mother and a pile of sports magazines for me; I gave my mother a jar of fancy soaps and Gerard a model aircraft carrier—the sort of thing he would have loved in the old days but now seemed sadly inappropriate. For each of us, my mother produced a big shopping bag full of stuff, shirts and sweaters, socks and underwear, a radio for me, a camera for my brother, all from the same department store and charged, I imagined, on a new account.

Now, with some real money in her pocket, she went to work. She sat at the kitchen table most of the next afternoon and paid bills, signing the checks, a pair of black drugstore reading glasses perched on her nose, biting her lip with awkward effort, just like William Bendix throwing a curveball in *The Babe Ruth Story*. When she was finished, she lay her pen down decisively, looking satisfied, like a president who'd just signed off on a treaty or some important legislation, savoring for once, I guess, the virtuous glow of the paid-in-full.

The next day I accompanied her to the phone-from-car located in the Signal Hills parking lot, where she used to transact her telephone business. I'd sat with her there a few times before, paged through a *Sporting News* while she talked to the people at the bank or the gas company, and it was a revelation. I had to admit it, she was good on the phone. She had gotten to know some people in billing and collection personally, asked for them by name, inquired about their children. Her voice took on a new quality, a slightly higher pitch. Suddenly she was more articulate. She drew on a vocabulary I'd never heard from her before, used words like "mortified" and "cognizant" and "forbearance," pronounced them all correctly as far as I knew, with a slightly schoolmarmish precision.

I could tell that people really liked her. I could hear the happy hum of their voices through the line, little bursts of laughter when my mother cracked a joke. With Janet at the bank she took to discussing house-plants. Seeing as the only green, growing thing in our house was mold, this struck me as sort of funny. But I kept my mouth shut, and as far as I could tell, my mother's advice was good.

It wasn't phony, my mother's lively telephone charm and chattiness, no more than good grammar and clean fingernails at a dinner party. Some women dressed up once a week and went out for lunch, but for my mother, this was it, her card party, her PTA, her ladies' night out—her chance, if not to shine, then just to get out for some adult company. Didn't matter that she was dressed in sweats, behind the wheel of a beat-up Plymouth, swollen and half benumbed. It didn't seem to matter that these weren't social calls, that their occasion were our financial difficulties.

She spent a long time on the line with Northwestern Bell that day, getting bounced from department to department, but she kept her cool. In those days, you didn't have to keep feeding the phone, so there was no hurry. At one point, a car full of high school kids pulled up behind us, and after a while, gave a short toot on the horn, not at all belligerent, just a polite reminder. I didn't think that I knew them but sank a little lower in my seat, just in case. When they beeped the horn again, my mother cradled the phone on her shoulder and made a gesture out the driver's side window. I don't think she actually flipped them the bird, but I believe that was her gist. She kept talking. The next time I looked, the kids were gone.

Finally, finally, she hung up. "Dial tone on Tuesday," she said.

I loved the sound of that, *dial tone*, something so definite and weighty and official about those two stressed syllables, like Mission Control talking about *lift-off*.

"Way to go, Mom," I said. "Another clutch performance."

She looked at me a little suspiciously, as if she weren't sure whether or not I was being a smart-aleck. But I meant it. Way to go, Mom.

Tuesday morning first thing I picked up the phone and sure enough, I heard it, dial tone, rich and reassuring, like a perfect C from a pitch pipe. My mother had insisted on a new, unlisted number, which made no sense to me at all, but I wasn't about to argue. I couldn't think of anybody to call, at least not at that hour, but I did dial the number for the correct time a couple of times, and listened to the recorded message, trying unsuccessfully to figure out whether the voice came from a real woman, or, as my brother had told me, was the product of some high-tech vocal synthesizer.

A few days after that, two guys from Sears showed up with a new hot-water heater, a sparkling white forty-gallon beauty they lugged down the basement and installed after an hour or so of wrench-rattling and pipe-banging. For the first time in nearly a year, we had something other than stove-top hot water. We checked the tap in the kitchen sink every five or minutes or so, waiting for the tank to heat.

"It's definitely warm now," Gerard said.

I stuck my hand in, too. "You call that warm?" I said. "It's hot."

Talk about simple pleasures. We took turns holding our hands under the faucet, just like Helen Keller. We made instant cocoa from the tap, two cups of soup that nobody touched, just to prove it could be done.

I took the first bath, a long, scalding soak. I stepped out of the tub—the mirror clouded, the whole bathroom thick with steam—feeling completely cooked, parboiled, pink and hideously wrinkled and unaccountably happy. At last, it seemed to me, things were getting better. We were on a roll. Anything was possible.

On New Year's Eve, George Walker stopped by our house. My mother was rattling around in the kitchen, off on another baking jag, having produced something like three or four separate dishes in the past couple of hours, all of them hors d'oeuvres, her most recent creation being what I believe were Pillsbury crescent rolls stuffed with molten cheese and peppers. (A lot of her best ideas, I think, came from recipes on the back and side panels of packages.) Gerard had left the house around seven, grousing to me that New Year's was amateur night, which is just what our father used to say. I was in the living room watching a minor bowl game, Liberty or Hula or Blue Bonnet, one of those, enjoying the spectacle of night football, the sound of it, play-by-play Muzak.

When I heard the knock, I went to the door and took a peek. Mr. Walker was standing on the front step, hatless, holding something in his arms, a long, flat cardboard box. I wasn't sure my mother would want me to open the door, but I did it anyway.

"Hi, Mr. Walker," I said.

He looked over my shoulder into the living room. "I hope I'm not disturbing you," he said.

"No," I said.

"Happy New Year," he said.

For me, it wasn't much of a holiday. Years ago, Gerard and I used to bang pots and pans and throw confetti; now it just felt like an extra Saturday night. But I didn't know about Mr. Walker. Underneath his overcoat, he was wearing a nice shirt. I wondered if he didn't used to go dancing with his wife on New Year's Eve. This had been his first Christmas without her.

"Same to you," I said.

"Here's a little something for your family," he said.

I took the box from him. It was one of those hickory-smoked beef and cheese gift packages—a couple of summer sausages big as nightsticks, blocks of cheddar and Monterey Jack, Edam and Gouda in red wax like hockey pucks, pancake mix, little vials of syrup, jam, the works.

"Where are your manners?" It was my mother, who'd come up behind me and was standing in the doorway, leaning on the frame.

"Thank you," I said.

"You're more than welcome," Mr. Walker said.

"You're too kind," my mother said.

I'm not sure why, but she looked all right. She was wearing a pair of slacks and one of Gerard's T-shirts, but at least it was clean. She looked different somehow, her hair pulled back in a new way possibly, maybe just combed. Or maybe it was just a new attitude. Maybe this is what she looked like when she lost her ornery edge, when she chose to be nice, maybe this was what her telephone voice looked like.

She chatted with Mr. Walker for a minute or so—the weather, a little bit of the year in review, very general—while I looked on, for whom adult small talk was still practically a foreign language, admiring their ability to keep the ball in the air.

"I won't shed a tear when this year passes," my mother said. " 'Good riddance,' I say."

"I couldn't agree more," Mr. Walker said.

"How about some *good* luck in the new year, Mr. Walker?" my mother said. "How about a lucky break?"

"I'm all for it, Mrs. Hawkins," he said. "Count me in."

In the storybook, Disney version of my life, it occurred to me, George Walker and my mother would become friends, and, after a rocky—and slightly zany—courtship, get married. It would be perfect. Both of them wounded in their way, lonely and wary, but still full of pluck and love for life, etc. United in their affection for me.

Mr. Walker checked his watch then. He wished my

mother good night, gave me a little salute, and then he made his exit.

As far as I could see, there were just a couple of problems with my story, happy ending-wise. An incurable degenerative nervous disorder with an ugly name, for one thing. Something awkward, potentially cute, and temporary would be better—a broken leg, say. My mother with a big cast and crutches—imagine the fun. How my brother was going to fit in would need to be worked out. And my father was a problem, too. All the single mothers in the after-school specials were widows, dearly departed dad just a benign framed photograph. That my father was very much alive and kept turning up at inconvenient times was going to be a problem, no doubt about it.

CHAPTER THIRTEEN

In the middle of a lesson about the justice system, I spotted Mrs. Oates hovering nervously outside our classroom door, peering through the narrow glass window, making timid waves in the direction of Mr. Baumgarten, who was fully engaged at the board with his three-color chalk representation of the branches of government.

In the past, Mrs. Oates had worked in the library and served as a kind of in-house, presumably uncertified, substitute teacher. Two years earlier, after Miss Miller had injured herself in an accident involving the paper cutter—sliced her finger clean off, the whisper went—Mrs. Oates took over our class in the afternoons for the remainder of the school year, splitting a shift with Mr. Bauer, the gym teacher, who wore his mesh shirt and whistle while he drilled us in geography and spelling. She was ill at ease in the classroom, though, apologetic and a little afraid of us—sixth graders can smell it, just like dogs—reduced finally to showing movies almost every afternoon, with the lights on. Now she worked in the office, answering the phone and typing letters for the principal, collecting tardy slips, doling out aspirin to sick kids.

I was in the back of the room with my buddies Chimera and Hauser, doodling in my notebook, crunching a cough drop. I just sat there, like everybody else, watching and waiting, while Mrs. Oates fluttered outside the door and Mr. B. droned on, enjoying the spectacle, I suppose, of perplexed, oblivious adults. But I had this feeling.

Eventually Mr. Baumgarten turned around. "Checks and balances," he was saying. "That's what it's all about. That's the beauty of it. Checks and balances."

I could see Patty Potter across the room nodding and grinning like an idiot, flushed with patriotism.

Mrs. Oates still hadn't knocked but finally she got Baumgarten's attention. He excused himself and stepped out. While they conferred quietly in the hall— Mrs. Oates pointing down the hall, Baumgarten nodding solemnly—I closed my notebook and started to gather up my things.

Mr. Baumgarten leaned back into the room and pointed at me. I heard the Grinch behind me, starting to chant, "You, you, you," but it didn't catch on, thank God. He was an asshole, everyone knew it.

"So long," Louie Chimera whispered. "It's been good to know you."

I gave Marty Hauser five and headed to the door.

"It's your father," Mr. B. said.

.   .   .

He was sitting in the office, paging through an abandoned Think-and-Do book. My father had always been a restless reader of anything—coverless magazines, catalogs, food labels, sugar packets, whatever was at hand, he'd read it.

He stood up and reached out to tousle my hair but the fact is he did it so awkwardly and the gesture was so out of character—no chucker of chins, my father—I may have flinched.

He was wearing a blue suit and white shirt open at the collar. There was a striped silk tie draped around his neck. He was wearing French cuffs, undone—folded back but no links. It was the middle of the afternoon. Whether he was partly dressed or undressed, coming or going, it wasn't clear. I remember noticing that the waxed shoelaces in his wing tips were untied.

This was the situation: He wanted to take me out of school for the day to attend to some unspecified family business. But the principal was out of the office—in the basement, Mrs. Oates thought, checking on the boiler—and she was reluctant to sign off on anything. Something irregular was going on, I'm sure she could sense it, something was not quite right. My father looked shady, even to me.

"Mr. Garraty should be back any minute," she said.

"I'm his father," he said, smiling. "For goodness sake. Do I need to show ID? I can do that. How many forms do you require?" he said, and reached for his wallet.

"Oh, no," Mrs. Oates said. She kept looking past him, watching the door, hoping to be delivered, I'm sure, staring so hard it was as if she were trying to make Mr. Garraty materialize through sheer force of will.

He turned to me. "Am I your father?"

I nodded and made a laughing sound.

"He's a chip," my father said. "Isn't he a chip? Right off the goddamned block."

My father and Mrs. Oates went back and forth a little while longer. She was deferential and stubborn, but my father was not a patient man. Finally he grabbed a piece of paper from her desk—it was that day's absentee list, a long purple list of mimeographed names—and turned it over. He produced a fountain pen from his pocket and uncapped it dramatically. He leaned over the desk, his hand circling in the air momentarily, warming up, and then he went to work. While he wrote, Mrs. Oates and I looked at each other. I don't believe I had ever stood so near to her before. She smelled like talcum powder. There was a little piece of Scotch tape on her glasses holding a tiny screw in place. Up close, she looked frail and sad. I could have spoken up then—whispered, mouthed something, shaken my head, something. But I didn't.

"There," my father said, and presented Mrs. Oates with the paper as if it were some kind of legal writ, a subpoena or a court order.

At the top of the page, I could see the words TO WHOM IT MAY CONCERN, written in oversize ornate script. Underneath there was a thick paragraph of text, all orbicular flourishes and curlicues, which I couldn't make out, and his flamboyant signature at the bottom, underlined. The whole thing reminded me of one of the replicas of the founding documents tacked onto Mr. B's bulletin board.

Mrs. Oates studied it, one hand on her eyeglasses, skeptical and impressed, both.

"Thank you, Mrs. Oates," my father said. "Give my best to Mr. Garraty," he said. He put his arm around me and swept me toward the door.

I looked back over my shoulder at Mrs. Oates, who was dialing her phone.

"See you tomorrow," I said.

We walked out of the office together, down the hall to my locker, where I grabbed my coat and an armload of books. My father had another big-ass car—a Newport with a push-button transmission—parked right out back. He opened the door for me and I got in. I sat there while he started the engine and fiddled with the heater vents, taking in the prospect of my school from the outside—the little kids' construction-paper snowmen plastered on the ground-floor windows, the rows and rows of classrooms all lit up, the big black clocks on the wall. On the second floor, I could see Baumgarten pacing back and forth in front of the windows, keeping an eye on the weather—business as usual. I used to be in there. And now, all of a sudden, on an overcast January afternoon, in the middle of the long gray stretch between Christmas and Easter, I'd been sprung loose, was out here, sitting in a strange car with my father, headed Lord-knows-where.

We drove down Smith Avenue into St. Paul. I sat in the

front seat, squeezed next to the passenger door, my hand on the latch. I wondered about my brother, where he was, whether or not my father had attempted to liberate him, too. I wondered where we were headed. But I didn't ask, and my father didn't offer anything. If I just hung on and waited, I figured, I would find out soon enough.

As we crossed the High Bridge—a rickety, narrow two-laner spanning the Mississippi—my father started feeling around under his seat for something. He kept one hand on the wheel, but his head was below the dash, and the car started to drift. Somebody honked, and he raised his head, jerked the wheel, and cursed. Then he went back to digging under the seat. The car meanwhile was edging closer and closer to the guardrail. I winced, waiting for the scraping of metal, sparks flying. I thought about grabbing the wheel. But just then, he straightened up, righted the car, and tossed something at me.

It was a baseball. I turned it in my hand and saw an autograph—Mickey Mantle's.

"Number seven," my father said.

It didn't look right. The pen had been skipping, for one thing, and the ink was smudged. Later, when I checked the autograph against the ones reproduced in my baseball magazines and yearbooks, it almost, but didn't quite match. There was something funny about the ball, too. It wasn't regulation. The laces were pale pink, not red, and it was just a shade too small—my hand knew it—like a British golf ball. It was made in China.

"What do you think?" he asked.

The Mick liked to drink (we know that now, don't we? The whole sad story), so maybe my father had run into him in a bar, and there, in a boozy hurry, he had autographed it with whatever was at hand, the best he could do under the circumstances. Maybe he was just a little bit under the weather when he signed it.

Maybe it really was genuine. Who knows? You just couldn't tell for sure.

"Incredible," I said. "Unbelievable."

My father made a flying, screeching turn onto West Seventh. He looked at me and smiled. I remembered how he had signed his name back in the principal's office, and it occurred to me that I might ask *him* to sign the ball. There was room for another autograph. But I didn't of course. I wanted his hands on the wheel, for one thing. Besides, he probably would have just laughed at me. Later, though, while I worked on my own autograph, filled line after line of my school notebooks, aiming for something worthy of being emblazoned on the barrel of a Louisville Slugger or printed across the palm of an A-2000, I borrowed that little flourish—my father's jaunty underscoring of his own name—and made it my own.

On the black-and-white TV hanging above the bar, Cronkite was soundlessly reading the news. He looked worried.

I was pressed into a corner booth, nursing a 7-Up, watching the molten wax pool up in the hurricane lamp in front of me, while my father stood with a group of men at the bar. He was shaking a black leather dice cup, laughing about something.

We'd been there—some downtown bar and grill, a chophouse, my father called it—for over an hour, maybe longer. It was hard to tell. It was a dark, smoky bunker that smelled of whiskey and fried onions. There was a row of framed celebrities on one wall—Milton Berle, Tony Bennett, Raymond Burr—and down a narrow hall leading to the kitchen, there was a cigarette machine and a pay phone.

My father had ordered us something to eat first thing, steak sandwiches and a couple of oversize onion rings delivered to our table in plastic baskets. He rubbed his hands together, miming A Famished Man, and never took a bite. I was hungry enough, but to me, cautious in the extreme when it came to food, who viewed meat loaf back then as an unnecessary and suspiciously complex form of ground beef, it looked utterly indigestible, the meat all fat and black gristle, the bread soggy with pink juice.

Charlie O'Connell had passed through maybe twenty minutes earlier, in constant convivial motion, shaking hands and slapping backs, making his hand into a pistol like a little kid, picking off friends across the room. He was on the water wagon, he announced, drinking only bitters, and allowed his glass to be inspected.

"You're a better man than me," my father told him.

Charlie O'Connell shook my hand. "So," he said. "We meet again." He tasted one of my onion rings. "Keep an eye on this old boy," he told me, and motioned to my father with his thumb. "Don't let him get into trouble."

Finally, my father returned with another round, 7-Up

for me, my third or fourth, and something the color of gasoline in a low-ball glass for himself, straight up. He'd started out drinking beer, the little ones—ponies—but switched over. Standing behind him was a guy in a plaid sport coat with a drink in his hand.

It was Tony Becker. He was a local sports personality, famous for—years ahead of his time—insulting the callers on his radio talk show. He wrote a column for a weekly newspaper, and when it rained during a Twins' telecast, he sat at a cardboard desk in the Calhoun Beach Hotel and read scores from around the league. Up close, in person, he looked soft, sort of puffed up, blotchy. He had a big, mindless smile on his face, which seemed free-floating, unconnected to anything at all. He looked like a happy balloon. He made no move to introduce himself; he simply stood there, looking down at me and beaming, exuding self-evident local celebrity.

I shifted my weight and started to stand but Tony Becker put his hand on my shoulder and jammed me back down. "So this is the ballplayer?" he asked my father. "The young Feller? The little ace?"

I wanted to explain that I was a first baseman, not a pitcher, but I never got a chance.

"The one and only," my father said.

"Kid got good stuff?"

"The best," my father said.

"I'm sure he does," Tony Becker said. "I'm sure he does." His hand was still on me, holding the back of my neck, under my shirt now, a moist, fleshy clamp. "How's his control?"

"Outstanding," my father said.

"You gotta have control," Tony Becker said. "Right, kid?"

"Sure," I said.

"He was undefeated last season," my father said. "Two no-hitters."

"Two?" Tony Becker said. "You don't say."

He punched me in the arm, hard, a knuckle working into the muscle somehow, some Marine Corps special-training kind of thing that hurt like hell.

"The kid can bring it," my father said.

I felt something hot and fluid working behind my eyes, a little burst pipe, but I didn't cry. Finally Tony Becker let go of me. Someone across the room was hollering at him, and he wandered off.

I looked at my father. He was red-faced and sweaty. I was hoping that he would say something, not apologize, maybe just explain, give me a chance to say that I understood. I had friends, I knew about bragging rights. It was okay, I would tell him. No hard feelings.

My father leaned across the table toward me and looked into the floor while he spoke toward my left ear.

"Listen, buddy," he said. "We gotta hit the road. Your grandmother is expecting us."

Twenty minutes later, my father—no hat, no gloves, no topcoat, shivering in his suit—and I were standing under a green street lamp outside his mother's house on Marshall Avenue, staring at a sad trunk full of groceries. There were cardboard flats of canned goods—cling peaches, wax beans, grapefruit juice, tuna, all off-brands—eight-packs of toilet paper, bags bulging with powdered milk and soda crackers, hand lotion and denture cleanser.

My grandmother was a severe, bookish woman, half blind in her old age, slight but sinewy. She was an atheist, and so was my father, the only ones I'd ever known. My mother was Roman Catholic, and before things fell apart, she would, from time to time, comb my brother's hair and tuck in my shirt and take us to mass, never consistently, but sometimes. Under father's religion on school forms, however, we learned to check "none." I always thought it would get me into trouble, but no one seemed to care. She insisted that we call her Nana. On birthdays, she sent savings bonds, impressive-looking nonmoney in small denominations. She'd raised two boys in the Depression, taught school for thirty years, and, my brother claimed, grown rich through shrewd investments in the stock market.

At Thanksgiving and Christmas, she used to sit on our living room couch, utterly motionless, her liver-spotted hands resting in her lap, her head slightly cocked. My mother fussed over her a little, offered her pillows and shawls, which she always refused, a glass of water, but mostly we ignored her. She sat there, practically invisible, but with a kind of lidless, reptilian watchfulness—I don't think she missed much.

I would dutifully sit next to her for a few minutes and make slow small talk in an overly loud voice (maybe she wasn't, but to me she *looked* hard of hearing). She was fond of English poetry, Milton especially—an odd choice for a nonbeliever, I know—which she used to quote without introduction. And so formal was her ordinary manner that I had a hard time recognizing that her iambic reflections on the human condition were in fact quotations, not just her offhand observations. "The mind is its own place," she would say, and I would nod and say, "Yes, Nana." "And in itself," she would tell me, "can make a Heaven of Hell, a Hell of Heaven."

I never knew her husband, my grandfather (what in the world would we have called *him*? I sometimes wondered). In the only photograph of him I'd ever seen, he looked stern and bristly—he was not about to smile for the camera, he thought it was nonsense, you could just tell. He was a railroad man, and when my father was just a little boy, he was killed in a train accident somewhere in Canada. My father's only sibling, an older brother, I was told, died in an automobile wreck at the age of eighteen.

They were a family of careless, accident-prone men, I'd always thought, which wasn't exactly true. Just a month before I'd learned that my father's brother, our uncle Gerard, for whom my brother was named, had, in fact, committed suicide: hanged himself with a belt in the basement of the house on Marshall Avenue, where my father, who was fourteen years old at the time, found him and cut him down with his pocketknife. The car crash was a fiction. Somehow my brother had known this for years.

"Come on," Gerard had said. "You didn't know that?"

There was a whole lot apparently that I didn't know, but I didn't like to let on. "Sure," I lied. It made me wonder about my grandfather—a train accident? what kind of accident?—and everything else I thought I knew.

When he still lived with us, before my mother got sick, my father every so often—a couple of times a year maybe—did his mother's grocery shopping. He'd piss and moan about having to do it for what seemed like hours before he'd finally go, and he always came home in a foul mood. One time I'd gone along with him, and it was almost funny. My father, pushing a cart through a crowded store, who couldn't tell the difference between lettuce and cabbage, cussing, squinting at his mother's tiny handwriting on the back of an envelope—she was nothing if not frugal—her list full of arrows and addenda and elaborate specs: brand and size, crushed tomatoes, not whole. There were warnings and angry exclamation points—she knew ahead of time exactly how he was going to go wrong. The wonder is that he did it at all, sometimes, however badly, however resentfully. As I say, he was not a patient man, certainly not one to be pinched too tightly by obligation.

"Okay, Sport," my father said. "Show time."

He hoisted a couple of bags into my arms and picked up three cardboard trays of canned goods with a grunt.

"Forward march," he said.

I was surprised to discover that my father would still bring his mother groceries. Like our basket of fruit and long, yellow check, it was another grand gesture, an irregular flourish, like buying everybody a round of drinks. This is what he did, I suppose, when he was feeling guilty or when other people's needs crossed his mind, which wasn't often.

Together, we made our way cautiously up the icy walk and onto the porch, single file, with me in the lead. I tripped the storm door latch with my elbow, and my father, cradling his cans perilously in one arm, fumbled with her key, which he kept on a special round ring, like a jailer's, and pushed the door open.

We stood in the vestibule stomping our feet. Nana's house was dim and crowded, full of furniture, maybe antique, maybe just old—rickety rockers, spindly legged highboys, glass-covered bookcases—the smell of liniment in the air. There were books everywhere, overflowing the shelves onto every surface, stacked precariously on the mantelpiece, piled on the floor, spilling out of cardboard cartons, filling the seat of a stuffed chair. It was as if she were living in the closed stacks—her whole life was in storage, and nothing circulated.

I could see her glasses glinting in the half-darkness. She was sitting on the couch, small and still as a chastened child.

My father nudged me forward. He didn't literally have me around the neck, cold steel pressed to my head, but I *felt* like a hostage, a human shield. He was scared of her, no doubt about it.

Finally she spoke, her voice like a creaking hinge. "When night darkens the streets," she said, "then wander forth the sons of Belial."

"Sorry so late, Ma," my father said. "I got tied up at the office."

"Flown with insolence and wine."

. . .

We unloaded the rest of the groceries from the car and deposited them in the tiny kitchen. It was pretty dismal: a yellowed linoleum floor worn down to the wood in spots, a scarred round oak table cluttered with newspapers and prescription bottles, a pull-chain light shining on the stained sink. It made me doubt Gerard's story about Nana's wealth—if she had money, why live like this?

She was standing there, her spindly legs wrapped in Ace bandages like World War I leggings, holding one of those old-fashioned long-handled grocery store gizmos for reaching things. It was as big as she was. She was arranging things on the upper shelves, making room. She was fierce, banging and rapping—as if she were mad at her dry goods, as if their disorder were a personal affront—but accurate. I had the feeling she could have dealt a hand of poker with that thing, dropped a dime into the coin slot of a pay phone.

Finally, she leaned it against the wall, and shuffled slowly across the room. She pulled one of the chairs out from the table, positioned it carefully, and sat down. My father stowed away groceries, and Nana barked at him, just a little. "*Creamed* corn," she said. "How many times have I got to tell you?" But her complaining seemed almost perfunctory, as if her heart weren't really in it.

Then she turned her attention to me. I'd been perched on the radiator, watching my father, trying to make myself inconspicuous. She said my name and pointed crookedly at the empty chair beside her.

She ask me whether I wanted a glass of milk. She offered me a Fig Newton, which is an old person's idea of a cookie.

"No thanks," I said.

Behind her metal glasses, her eyes were milky and a little vague—I might have just been a dark shape to her, another shadow. But it was benign, practically kindly attention she was giving me, I think. I think she still had some hopes for me.

"Your father tells me that you are a lover of baseball," she said. "A fanatic."

"A little," I said. "A little fanatic."

She made some remarks about the Series, and it was clear to me that she knew what she was talking about. Gibson was masterful on the mound, she said, Brock wonderfully swift-footed. She asked me what I thought of the Twins' off-season maneuvering, their prospects for next year. She must have been reading the sports page, whether simply out of curiosity or in anticipation of a conversation with me, I have no idea. It sounded as if she'd been studying baseball, like a new course she was working up, memorizing its forms, mastering the discourse, the names and the idiom, teaching herself to talk the talk.

Still, she talked baseball like a second language, with an accent. "The bullpen," she said, "has been particularly tragic."

"They need a left-hander," I said.

"This new fellow," she said, "acquired on waivers. What about him?"

"Nothing special," I said. "A ham-and-egger."

"What?" she said. She cocked her head.

"He's inconsistent," I said. "On-again, off again."

"What did you call him?" She asked. "What's the term?"

I said it again slowly. "A ham-and-egger."

She turned to my father. He was holding a box of Uncle Ben's, glaring at me. "Yes," she said. "Of course."

We didn't linger much after that. Nana asked me about my mother and Gerard, and I told her that they were fine. She seemed to believe me, and it made me wonder what my father had been telling her about our home life, what sort of fiction he'd spun for her. According to him, I threw no-hitters, so who knows, maybe Gerard was an Eagle Scout, maybe he and my mother were Ozzie and Harriet.

Nana handed my father a handful of crumpled cash to cover the groceries and walked with us to the front door, clinging to my arm. She stood still while I kissed her, as always, on the cheek, her fragile, translucent-looking skin impossibly soft against my lips, like some rare and delicate fabric.

"Thank you," she said. "Now be careful."

There was a thin layer of icy snow coating the car. My father scraped at the window a little with a credit card and then gave up. He turned on the wipers, which were frozen in place, and then the defroster. But he didn't wait for the windows to clear.

We headed down Dayton toward downtown. He lit a cigarette and took a long drag. He turned the radio on, punched some buttons, and turned it off. He rapped his knuckles on the steering wheel. He was all nervous, hunched urgency. What he wanted, I knew, was a drink, right now. I could practically smell his need. I wanted to go home. I was hoping he would drop me off first, but I didn't dare ask. He ran a four-way stop and snorted his contempt, I imagined, for the pettiness of the law-abiding.

When he finally said something, we were just passing the Cathedral. Through the iced-over window, I could see it only dimly. At night, dark and deserted, it spooked me, the cold gray stone and stained glass, shadowy statuary, the winding sidewalk paths leading who-knows-where. It was a bad neighborhood now, and the Cathedral itself had become a haven for homeless men, who snored in the back pews, and when the church was locked, gathered in the doorways, raggedy and hollow-eyed. We were too close to see the dome, but I knew it was there, I could feel it, green copper looming in the night sky.

"Tell me what I am," my father said. He dropped his butt on the floor and stomped it. "Tell me, smart ass."

"Dad," I said.

He was going too fast. There were safety belts in the car, but back then, nobody used them. Still I clung irrationally to a loose strap, wrapped it tight around my wrist, desperately reining in nothing at all.

"A ham-and-egger?" he said. "Is that what I am? A ham-and-fucking-egger?" He cuffed me then, back-handed, good and hard, under the chin. My head snapped back against the seat, and I left it there. I closed my eyes and waited. If he was going to hit me again, I didn't want to see it coming.

My father lit another cigarette then—I could hear the scrape of the match, a tiny explosion, I could smell the sulfur—and I thought, okay. He's done with me.

That's when I heard it, a dull, hollow-sounding thud. I felt it, too, a tremor on the passenger side. We'd hit something—not another car, it wasn't a metallic sound—something big with some give, something massy and soft, collapsible.

I looked at my father. He braked now, too late, and the car started to fishtail. He spun the wheel, let off the brake, and righted the car. He glanced in the mirror, but he kept going, his mouth set, his hands gripping the wheel tight.

I turned and looked back over my shoulder and saw—what? Call it a shape, a form, something, something lying in the road. It might have been a dog or a trash can.

"What?" my father said. "What?"

I could see his face, illuminated by the light of the dash, turned toward me, waiting.

"Nothing," I said.

. . .

That night I lay in bed a long time thinking about that sound. My father was a hit-and-run driver. That's who he is, I thought. If someone or something got in his way, he ran it over. He destroyed things, and he never looked back.

I was still awake after midnight when my brother came home stinking of cigarettes and beer. He fell into bed with his clothes on and started snoring. I lay perfectly still and kept quiet, watching reflected headlights flash across the bedroom wall when a car drove down our street, listening, waiting. Sweet dreams, my mother had said. May you die in your sleep.

CHAPTER FOURTEEN

I'd been shoveling snow for Mr. Walker that winter. He had two gleaming shovels, one for lifting, one for pushing snow down the long straightaway of his driveway. I chopped ice and spread rock salt, which he bought in quantity and stored in a barrel in the garage.

I'd not breathed a word to anyone about my afternoon with my father at the bar and our visit to Nana's. What I would have wanted to get across couldn't really be put into words: Tony Becker's stupid smile, his clammy hand on the back of my neck; my grandmother's parchment skin, her bottles of pills, her metal grabber; the sound of my father's car slamming into whatever it was we hit, the back of his hand across my face. It was unutterable. I could have only gestured in its general direction. Maybe Gerard had been likewise spirited away at some time, maybe he'd done the grocery run himself. I wondered if my father had ever roughed him up at all. But I would never know. My brother had his secrets, and I had mine.

After shoveling snow, we'd sit at the kitchen table.

Mr. Walker boiled water, and while I drank hot chocolate, he'd stir up a murky cup of instant Folger's for himself. We talked about snowblowers, pros and cons, and together we staked out a kind of wait-and-see position—to be honest, neither of us was especially eager to start fooling around with some murderously sharp piece of self-propelled machinery. We stared out the window together, past the snowbanks, and counted the days until pitchers and catchers reported.

It was during one of those hot-stove chats—late January, my hat and gloves warming on the radiator, steam rising from our mugs—that the subject of high school came up. Mr. Walker knew my grades and test scores were good, he'd done some checking. The public school was fine, of course—he taught there, after all—but there were other possibilities. Had I given it any thought? Mr. Walker himself was a graduate of a local private school for boys, an academy.

Of course I knew all about the academy. I'd watched their football team demolish our local public school boys the fall before in a preseason game. I remember them taking the field like Ohio State or Notre Dame, helmets gleaming, an endless swarming squad, like the Roman legions. While our guys did their headbanging, kill-kill warm-up in one end zone, the academy players performed silent calisthenics, like a precision drill team, a show of military discipline and controlled power, no rah-rah bullshit, just hands slapping pads and cleats hitting the turf in perfect unison, an ominous drumbeat. They were winners, and they knew it.

A family down the block from us had sent their two

sons to the academy, and I used to see them walk past
our house in their blue uniforms and shiny black shoes.
They seemed like members of some obscure youth
branch of the armed service or new order of scouts, if
not literally Boy Scouts, then at least redolent of that
particular blend of civic virtue, achievement, and personal hygiene.

Whose idea was it? I don't know anymore. Maybe
Mr. Walker suggested it, made mention in passing,
threw out a possibility, some conditional construction,
a wish. He ran it up the flagpole. Wouldn't it be nice?
But I seized on it, grabbed hold. I took the merest hint,
fleshed it out and colored it in, adding depth and shade,
until I had created something more substantial than a
fantasy, more vivid than a daydream, something that
seemed real and ready-made, an entire life of happy
belonging and orderly, progressive achievement—a story
for me to star in.

One thing led to another. Pretty soon Mr. Walker's
yearbooks were spread out across the kitchen table. In
his graduation picture, young George Walker wore
heavy black glasses, a badly knotted tie, and an expression of forced geniality—just like at the wake, the same
sorrowful smile exactly. He had lots of hair back then,
combed straight back in slick wavy ridges. Under his
name it said Porgie, Specs, Ace, Big Train, Bound for
Glory.

In the baseball photos, he looked more like himself,
at ease, standing in the back row of the team photo,
properly capped, a little cocky even. There was an individual shot of him, clasping three baseballs in his big

hand, extending them toward the camera with a goofy grin on his face—a classic pitcher's pose, just the way I'd seen Raschi and Feller, Whitey Ford and Sudden Sam McDowell. It was obvious he was a star.

I got Mr. Walker talking, and before long, I could name the 1939 varsity starting lineup. He told me who was who and described their baseball personalities, gave me the real lowdown—who had power but no wheels, who could throw smoke, who knew how to lay one down and could hit behind a runner, who couldn't hit a lick, who had rabbit ears and was not to be trusted on the bases. I knew they were probably fat and old now, bald and arthritic, a bunch of bankers, maybe dead, but still. These black-and-white guys in their baggy woolens—he called them Stinky and Birdman, Honus, Hamster, and Dingle—seemed more vivid and interesting to me, more real somehow, than my own teammates or even the current batch of full-color, double-knit professional stars I watched on television.

I studied the pictures of the gray and chiseled headmaster, who seemed stern but kindly. My father would never get past *him*, I imagined. I looked at the photographs of students, too, candids of them—in the lab, staring into a beaker, in the library, leaning over a drawer in the card catalog—and I imagined myself in their place, uniformed and studious. It was like catalog shopping, for a whole new life of safety and certainty.

I read about clubs and student activities and recognized which extracurriculars were for losers—the debating society, glee club, rifle team—and which ones were worthy of aspiring to. Mr. Walker schooled me on the best teachers, whose homeroom was the best, and right then, at his kitchen table, it all seemed almost plausible.

Finally, I said something about tuition. There were scholarships, Mr. Walker told me. Work-study. A boy who was deserving could get help. All I had to do was take the entrance exam and fill out an application.

"What about my mom?" I said. "She'd never let me."

"I'll talk to her," he said. "I'll give it a shot."

There was a pause then, a full stop, Mr. Walker blinking behind his big glasses, realizing, I think, what he'd actually promised, knowing it still wasn't too late to wiggle out of it—to clear his throat and amend himself, to clarify and qualify—and I expected him to do just that. But he didn't. He just smiled weakly and cleared the dishes. The man made a promise to a boy, swallowed hard, and kept it. Give him credit.

I told my brother about it. We were lying in our bunks listening to Tony Becker badmouth Muhammad Ali on his call-in show. We loved Ali, Gerard and I—his half-berserk bravado, his rhyming predictions, his fancy footwork. After he'd been stripped of the title, we watched a replay of the Zora Folley fight on *Wide World of Sports*. Afterward, my brother had caught me flicking jabs at the mirror. I wanted Ali's graceful power, his speed, his poetry.

"Give it up," Gerard told me.

He knew some academy boys, and he despised them, every one. They lived in Edina and Highland Park. They played tennis and golf; the school's parking lot was full of sports cars. My brother resented their trim good looks, their deck shoes and car stereos, their orthodontic and dermatological appointments, their perfect parents, their conference championships year after year. All that unearned good fortune galled him, sure. Were *they* deserving?

"They're candy-asses," he said, and fired up a cigarette. "Candy-asses and cake-eaters."

"Mr. Walker thinks I can get financial aid," I said. "A scholarship."

"I'm sure you will," he said.

He had a feeling—we both did, don't ask me how, we just did—that it was going to happen. His little brother was going to eat cake. He exhaled and sent a wispy, badly formed smoke ring floating eerily toward the ceiling.

"Maybe you could transfer," I said.

But I knew he wouldn't. For all his native smarts, Gerard, I was afraid, had lost interest in school. Given up. He used to be in all the accelerated sections, but he'd dropped them, one by one. "It's all bullshit," he'd say. "Mickey Mouse." Now he'd go weeks without taking a book home. He didn't seem to care anymore.

"Sure," he said.

Gerard turned over heavily, and the bed wobbled a little. On the radio, Tony Becker was still ranting about Ali—draft dodger, un-American, he was a blot, a blight, disgraceful and disloyal. He called him Gaseous Cassius. I was half hoping Gerard would call me some names, slug me maybe, like old times. But he wouldn't do it.

I could feel his unhappy weight shifting beneath me, a human anchor, pulling me down. It *wasn't* fair, I knew. But I didn't know what I was supposed to do about it.

I came from school one afternoon and found Mr. Walker sitting in the living room with my mother. He was pitching the academy to her. The coffee table was littered with the usual domestic debris—pop cans, newspapers, advertising circulars and unopened junk mail, dirty dishes—but one corner had been cleared off, and there, between them, sat a big pile of glossy literature, pamphlets full of color pictures: smiling students, a brand new gym, spacious grounds. Under the trees, there were students in navy pants and oxford shirts reading books, strumming guitars, playing chess. There was a lake for chrissake, kids in canoes.

My mother was leaning forward, arms crossed and balanced on the head of her cane, taking it all in, looking neither especially impressed nor cynical, just coolly attentive. It was weird seeing them together like that, in conference, such an unlikely summit. It made me feel a little uneasy, this not-quite intimacy.

Mr. Walker nodded at me and kept talking, about academic excellence—small classes and personal attention, first-rate facilities, all those expensive buzzwords. There were accelerated courses and after-school tutoring sessions, he said. He quoted some statistics about national merit scholars and college placement.

"It's a wonderful opportunity for a bright student," he said.

Mr. Walker must have sensed somehow that my mother might be susceptible to the appeal of educational opportunity. She'd been a bright student herself, proud of the fact that she'd known how to read even before she started school and had skipped a grade—third or fourth, I can't remember which. But after high school, she went right to work—college just wasn't in the cards for her, no matter how smart she was, I guess—at Brown and Bigelow, first as a secretary, then as an office manager. (That's where she'd met my father: She'd hired him for the all-night cleaning crew.) Still, she took night classes—shorthand, bookkeeping.

When my brother and I were small, just starting school, she used to come home from St. Paul Book and Stationery with armloads of educational stuff, chemistry sets and telescopes, school-quality maps, volumes of illustrated classics. Even after my father left, she kept bringing home the give-away first volume of grocery-store encyclopedias, so that with those freebies lying around the house, Gerard and I became disproportionately knowledgeable regarding subjects at the front of the alphabet—John Adams and Alfred the Great, Aztecs and astronomy.

"This is a school for rich kids," she said. "Isn't that true?"

Next to Mr. Walker, my mother seemed smaller, not frail, but strategically diminished somehow, warily compact, coiled.

"Not really," Mr. Walker said.

"Mr. Walker thinks that I could get a scholarship," I said.

"Based on what?" my mother said.

"Need, for one thing," Mr. Walker said.

"We've got that," my mother said. "Maybe you've noticed. We're up to our eyebrows in need. We're leading the league in that particular category."

"Merit, too," Mr. Walker said. "Harlan's grades are outstanding. If he does well on the entrance exam—"

"He'll do well," my mother said.

"Of course he will," Mr. Walker said.

"And you're going to help?"

"I'll do whatever I can. I can write a recommendation."

"The uniforms," she said. "Who pays for them?"

Mr. Walker cleared his throat and made some reassuring noise about incidental expenses—uniforms, lab fees, books—being included in the financial aid package, which I couldn't help but think of literally, as a little container, a kit.

"The first step," Mr. Walker said, "is to take the test. That's free."

My mother looked at me and motioned toward the table. "This?" she said. "You want this?" She knew damn well I did—who wouldn't?—but she was going to make me say it.

We both knew I had no business in a prep school. Sure, if things had been different, I might have been headed there, might have taken my place with a bunch of other lawyers' and doctors' kids and fit right in, if my mother had not gotten sick, if there had been no divorce, if my father hadn't welshed on child support— if, if, if. But now? Who was I kidding? I didn't belong in a canoe. I slept in my clothes and ate cereal for dinner. What in the world were they going to prepare *me* for?

"Yes," I said.

My mother smiled woodenly at me with what I took to be sad foreknowledge. But I'm just guessing. Maybe it was something else altogether, part mockery, part resignation.

"Are you sure?" she said.

"Sure," I said. "I'm sure."

"Go ahead and take the test then," she said, and pushed back from the table, like a poker player folding and getting ready to cash in. "Good luck."

Things just unraveled after that. I thanked Mr. Walker, and Mr. Walker thanked my mother. She grabbed her cane and hoisted herself, slowly and awkwardly, wheezing a little, and when she bumped the edge of the table and knocked one of the academy brochures onto the floor, nobody bent to pick it up. We just let it lie.

CHAPTER FIFTEEN

A few days later, out of the blue, my brother started making inquiries about my baseball cards. Of course I was suspicious. When he came in the room, I was lying on my bed doing my English homework, dutifully writing out answers to the discussion questions for "The Most Dangerous Game." *What forces within himself must Rainsford keep in check in order to survive? Do people like Zaroff really exist—people who feel superior to and exempt from social norms and are indifferent to human suffering? Do you agree that "evil is a tangible thing"?* I thought he was going to give me some grief about studying. My schoolwork was like a vicious habit I indulged only in private—I rarely got caught in the act. Instead he started asking me questions. He wanted to know about different sets, my oldest card, rarities and misprints. I dragged my card box out of the closet—it was huge, a battered cardboard carton—and fished around for some things that might impress him.

I showed him my 1964 card of Ken Hubbs, the Cubs second baseman killed in an off-season plane crash.

IN MEMORIAM was printed across the card in black letters, presumably a last-minute addition. Kenny looked pale and pasty underneath his blue batting helmet, practically dead already, sick with fright, doomed.

"Was he any good?" Gerard wanted to know.

"Rookie of the year," I said.

I showed him a rubber-banded pack of replica old-timer's cards, which I bought from a vending machine at the state fair: leather-faced Honus Wagner; Paul and Lloyd Waner, Big Poison and Little Poison; Christy Mathewson clutching a ball in his tiny glove; Walter Johnson with his windmill arms and sweet Christian countenance; crazy old pinch-faced, spike-sharpening Ty Cobb. I loved the old guys, the dirt eaters; they were like pioneer ancestors in a family album, severe and heroic.

"Ty Cobb?" Gerard said. "You have Ty Cobb?"

"It's a reprint," I said. "A facsimile."

"Oh," he said.

Gerard put a cigarette in his mouth and took a lighter from his shirt pocket. It was clear, glass or plastic, and there was a feathery orange fishing lure in the fluid, floating, like a specimen.

Sometime that winter I noticed that he had started acquiring expensive-looking objects. Some of it was small, smart gadgetry, like the cigarette lighter—a compass, a pocketknife complete with a corkscrew and a miniature removable tweezers and toothpick. It seemed like dad stuff, the paraphernalia of manhood. These things were all compact and well made, substantial, weighty. When he wasn't around, I would pick them up and hold them—I did it guiltily, as if I were fingering museum artifacts—and feel a certain charge of pleasure, a sensual delight in their solidity and precision.

It was a mystery. Where'd these things come from? Where'd he get the money? His job at the drugstore paid minimum wage. There were no sales slips, no store bags. It worried me to think that he might be stealing. Gerard didn't strike me as especially deft or light-fingered. He was the kind of guy who got caught. What would my brother want with this kind of stuff? I tried to imagine him on some sort of wilderness expedition, tracking true north on some godforsaken tundra with the help of his trusty compass, reading a map in the frozen cold under the flame of his lighter.

I showed him some of the special issue cards Topps put out each year, usually just pictures of a couple of players clowning around, with hokey headlines, which I loved: TRIBE THUMPERS (Rocky Colavito and Leon Wagner), RIVAL FENCE BUSTERS (Willie Mays and Duke Snider), our own owns TWIN TERRORS (Killebrew and Allison), and a host of others—GIANT GUNNERS, FRIENDLY FOES, PITCHERS BEWARE! I pointed to Dick Stuart, Roberto Clemente, and Willie Stargell, three Pittsburgh Pirate sluggers brandishing their bats at the camera. "Corsair Trio," I said.

"Sounds like the name of a band," Gerard said.

I didn't believe for a minute that Gerard's interest was sincere, but still, I liked the attention. Every day old people get swindled, hand over their savings happily to con men who earn their gratitude—not trust—just by paying attention to them, looking at the photos of their grandchildren, their houseplants, their homemade ornaments, their mangy cats and sleepy dogs. They look and listen and fill lonely people with the sense that there may be something remarkable about their things and about them. That's what it felt like. I knew damn well my brother wasn't really interested. I knew he wanted something from me. He was the guy who trashed my Tony Oliva. But still. I was grateful.

He listened while I explained how Dick Ellsworth, the Cubs pitcher, who was really left-handed, posed for his baseball card photo the year before as a righty, and Joe Koppe, the Angels' second-string shortstop and another smart aleck, right-handed like all infielders, posed as a lefty.

"Very funny," Gerard said.

I pulled out some of the cards from the '50s that Jerry Wozniak, who lived down the block and knew I collected, gave me before he left for basic training—Ted Williams, smiling like a man who was the greatest hitter who ever lived and knew it; a skinny Harmon Killebrew, still on the Senators; Joe Garagiola the broadcaster, a catcher for the Pirates; and Chuck Connors, the Rifleman, a first baseman for the Dodgers.

"I know a guy who buys cards," Gerard said.

"Really," I said.

"He pays cash."

"If we bring him some cards," Gerard said, "he'll look them over, tell us what they're worth. Appraise them. Aren't you curious?"

"I don't know," I said.

"Come on," Gerard said. "You might really have something. What do you say?"

"I'll think about it," I said.

The next Saturday my brother and I took a number five bus downtown, the Como-Stryker, which my mother used to say sounded like the name of a serial killer. I had a manila envelope stuffed fat with baseball cards on my lap. Gerard had stood over my shoulder the night before while I picked out the cards to bring in.

"Forget the common players," he said. "Just stars. Mantle and Mays. Koufax and Drysdale. Banks. Musial. Gibson."

Gerard's litany slowed down then—he really wasn't much of a fan. It was like he was naming the presidents. "Kaline," he said. "Aaron."

"Aaron who?" I'd said.

"Screw you," he'd said. "Don't forget what's-his-name. The dead guy."

We didn't say much on the bus. I watched Gerard fiddle with a new key chain—a big brass ring with a silver dollar impaled on it. I'd heard it was illegal to deface coins—pennies on the railroad track and all that—but I wasn't about to say anything. His jaw was thick, his face still meaty, but it had more definition somehow. He looked older, harder.

I had agreed to go to the card shop in part because I liked the idea of us doing something together. I must have imagined some sort of chummy outing. It had been a while since our early morning skating, and I would have loved to have recaptured that feeling of silent togetherness. But we were ill at ease and semi-surly with each other, out of habit, I guess, just like always. I stared out the window, and my brother rubbed his key-chain dollar, like he was polishing it. We weren't really that different, it occurred to me, him with his gadgets, me with my cards, both of us piling stuff up. We were both collectors at heart.

"If you sell something," Gerard said finally as we stepped off the bus, "you cut me in, right? Finder's fee, sales commission, you know. A little something off the top. For services rendered. We both make out."

"For services rendered," I said.

"Fair is fair," he said.

The store was a newsstand really, with big piles of fat Sunday papers from around the country stacked in front along with racks of magazines. There was a fish-bowl full of some questionable-looking candy on the counter, boxes full of comic books stored in plastic bags.

Danny Sellers, my brother's friend, was sitting on a wooden stool at the register, a bottle of orange soda in one hand, a magazine in the other. They made some barking noise at each other, guttural variations on their names, I think, some kind of secret verbal handshake.

"The boss is here," Danny said. "I'll go get him."

In the back of the store, there was a step and a rickety wooden turnstile with a hand-lettered sign taped to it: YOU MUST BE EIGHTEEN TO GO BEYOND THIS POINT. Up there, I knew, were the dirty books.

Gerard caught me craning my neck. "Don't look," he said. "You'll go blind."

On display in a locked glass case, there were individual baseball cards, like Swiss watches in a jewelry store. It depressed me a little, I don't why. There were cards I owned in the case, but there, stickered with price tags, under glass, they looked sterile and sad. It's funny, I know, but those pristine, perfectly preserved cards, the ones in the mint condition, with their sharp corners, their bright images, their shiny surfaces, looked false to me somehow, like counterfeits, like knock-offs of my battered, well-worn originals.

A few minutes later, the guy who bought baseball cards emerged from a back room. His name was Rossi. According to Danny Sellers, he was loaded—he carried a fat wallet filled with fifty-dollar bills.

"Greetings, gentleman," he said. "What can I do for you?"

He must have been in his mid-thirties, long-haired and moustached, wearing a jean jacket over a Tweety Bird T-shirt. He looked a little like Sonny Bono. I handed my brother the envelope of cards and stepped back.

"We've got some baseball cards," Gerard said. "Some good ones. We thought you might be interested."

"Might be? Might be? Of course, I'm interested," Rossi said. "Let's see what you got. Let's have a look."

When he spoke, he generated just the slightest bit of white froth at the corners of his mouth, tiny saliva-suds, not repulsive exactly, but something you couldn't help but notice.

I picked up a *Time*—there was a flat-nosed, glowering Soviet admiral on the cover with a collar full of gold braid—and leafed through it, keeping one eye on Rossi. He took each card in hand, one by one, and examined it front and back. Some he held up to the light and turned sideways. He was slow and methodical. When he was done with each card, he gently added it to a neat stack he was forming on the counter. Gerard and Danny Sellers were watching him, trying to read him, I think, seeing if they could gauge his interest.

This was about the time card collecting first started to be pursued as a serious hobby, when the price guides began to appear—cheap stapled booklets full of closely printed columns of numbers, like tax tables. In a few years kids with magnifying glasses would be talking to each other about sharp corners, grading each other's cards—mint, near mint, excellent, very good.

Rossi shook the last couple of cards from the envelope. Gerard looked at me with a big smile on his face and rubbed his thumb and fingers together. He was looking forward to seeing some of those famous fifties in Rossi's wallet. I wondered why exactly Gerard was so keen on scoring some quick cash, why he so obviously wanted something right now. Maybe he just wanted beer money, maybe he wanted to buy some new gadget. Probably he just wanted to indulge some new, more expensive bad habit. I just hoped he wasn't in some kind of trouble. If he needed help, really needed it, I'd have sold my cards, every one of them.

The trouble was this. My favorites were all faded and bent, creased, frayed around the corners. Some were fat with moisture, smelled of mildew, stained with my greasy fingerprints. I'd never clothespinned them to the spokes of my bike or anything like that, but still, I gave them a beating. I used to flip cards during recess on the playground with my grade-school buddies. I sorted them endlessly, studied the statistics on the back, lined them up for the game of the week. I carried them in the pockets of my jeans and push-pinned some to my bulletin board. I knew that Rossi wouldn't want any of my cards for his glass case. I knew that I could never be a serious collector—I was too rough on the things I loved. Simple as that.

We didn't say much on the way home. Gerard was pissed, and I couldn't really blame him. He'd come a long way for nothing. He had high hopes. I was a little bit disappointed, too, but mostly relieved.

As the bus headed over the Wabasha Bridge, I pulled a handful of cards from the envelope and read the backs. Cesar Tovar was born in Caracas, Venezuela. Mickey Mantle's real name was Mickey Mantle. In the off-season, Harmon Killebrew liked to watched television. Roger Maris had the same birthday as my mother.

Gerard elbowed me. "You heard him," he said. "They're worthless."

"I know."

"You're wasting your time," my brother said.

"Maybe," I said.

CHAPTER SIXTEEN

On the morning of the academy entrance exam, I waited quietly at the door for Mr. Walker, who had offered to accompany me. It was the first Saturday in March, the weekend of the high school hockey tournament. Gerard had gotten up, drunk a quart of orange juice, and sunk back into bed. My mother was sitting on the couch, looking down through her drugstore reading glasses at the sports page. She looked unusually pensive, almost scholarly.

"I like the kids from the Range," she said.

Since her meeting with Mr. Walker, neither of us had said anything about the academy. I understood that one of the unspoken conditions of my being allowed to take the test was that I shut up about it, keep it to myself. Which was fine by me. My imaginings were largely sensory and imagistic anyway: a sparkling lake, wool uniforms, a team photo—the props, costume, and supporting cast. I don't know what I would have *said* about it.

Mr. Walker's car pulled up then, and he gave a short beep. I glanced at my mother and paused, wondering whether one of us shouldn't say something. She looked up from the paper then, and the left side of her face twitched suddenly, like something almost involuntary, a spasm—a quick grimacing wink.

We stopped for breakfast at a drugstore lunch counter where the waitress knew Mr. Walker and how he liked his eggs. I ordered pancakes, and we sat there together in a corner booth passing a newspaper back and forth.

Mr. Walker seemed nervous. *He* was dressed up, for one thing, which made me nervous. He was wearing a knit tie and a navy sweater vest, for once looking exactly like a history teacher. And he kept checking his watch, sneaking a glance every couple of bites.

That was when it hit me, really hit me, that what I was headed for was not some ceremonial swearing-in, not an induction or an initiation. It was a test. There were going to be word problems, parallel lines cut by a transversal, synonyms and antonyms, little boxes to be folded. All of the above, none of the above. There were going to be right answers and wrong answers, a penalty for guessing.

"I like the kids from the Range," I told Mr. Walker.

He had gone out on a limb for me, sold my mother the package—his hopes were up—and if I choked now, he was going to be embarrassed and disappointed.

"Me too," Mr. Walker said, and nodded gravely as he stole another peek at his watch.

At the academy, with almost an hour still to kill, we walked around the main building, which in its vast and sparkling emptiness seemed to me more like a museum than a school. We walked solemnly down the endless halls, and I whispered my admiration. I was afraid to raise my voice. We peered into a darkened science lab full of microscopes and beakers and shelves of specimens, the periodic table plastered on one wall, a giant slide rule hanging above the blackboard. We stepped inside the new gym, a blinding waxed wonder, and on the way out, stood for a long time in front of the mirrored trophy case in the vestibule, where the hardware stretched infinitely, plaques and pennants and silver cups, trophies adorned with eagles and little statues, like figurines on a cake, only golden, miniature, quaintly dated players each frozen in an archetypal act: aiming a set shot, stiff-arming a tackler, swinging from the heels. There were a couple of footballs painted with scores, some frayed basketball netting, and one slightly yellowed autographed baseball that I imagined was from Mr. Walker's era.

While Mr. Walker ducked into a men's room—his second trip since we'd arrived at the academy—I wandered the halls and read bulletin boards. There was going to be a father-son pancake breakfast on Sunday. The Mothers Club silent auction was at the end of the month, and there was a picture of its organizers—a trio of smiling, helmet-haired mothers, all blonde Doris Day look-alikes.

I looked out a window at the fields behind the school—now, in March, a vast, mostly snow-covered expanse. But I could see a backstop and bleachers. I imagined young George Walker out there, standing on the mound, toeing the rubber and peering in for the sign, the Big Train getting ready to leave the station. I tried to imagine myself at first base, on my toes, crouched and ready, but somehow, I couldn't quite bring it into focus. It was like trying to watch something on our lousy TV—all you could pull in was a faint and flickering image, a snowy screen full of shadows.

I looked around the bookstore. There were three men chatting near the register, paper coffee cups in hand, two of whom I knew were academy instructors—the guys who taught Spanish and chemistry. Having recognized them from their pictures in Mr. Walker's yearbook—it must have been basically the same faculty, aged twenty-years—I felt intimidated by them in the flesh. Because I had encountered them first in photographs, they seemed famous to me. I felt a little sorry for them, too, so sadly diminished did they seem from their more robust, younger and dark-haired selves.

In the back of the store, I found the freshman textbooks. There was a huge hardback anthology called *The Human Experience*—poetry, fiction, and drama, all in one. In the back of the book there was a glossary of literary terms along with a concise guide to writing research papers. *Earth Science* was even bigger, full of rock and mineral tables, topographic maps, explanations of soil composition and rock formation and the water cycle, earthquakes and volcanoes, and came with a matching paperback workbook with perforated pages. It didn't look that hard. I could fill in the blanks as well as anybody. Higher math, on the other hand, scared me a little—my brother used to jazz me from time to time with talk about sines and cosines, irrational numbers, *imaginary* numbers, just you wait, he'd say and smile— but even the algebra book began with a reassuringly commonsensical discussion of set theory. In a history text there was a chapter on each of the world's great civilizations, lots of illustrations, colorful timelines and numbered checklists of essential points, boxed biographies of important figures, Hammurabi, Nefertiti, Pericles, Hannibal, like historical bubble gum cards—name, head shot, and career highlights.

I liked holding those books, the smell of them, the satisfyingly solid weight of a good year's worth of learning. What I held, of course, was just the promise of knowledge, the idea of it, not the thing itself. All the complexity had been smoothed over, the contradictions and confusion extracted. Here was knowledge as smooth and sweet as a milkshake. Even then I knew it was false, but I loved it anyway, because it was so wonderfully false.

Finally, it was time. We signed in at the office, where a woman checked my name off her list and pointed me toward the cafeteria. Mr. Walker wished me luck and said he'd meet me afterward. I stepped inside and stood for a moment to get my bearings. Other kids brushed by me, entering in groups of two and three, old friends apparently, casual as can be, talking and laughing, just hanging out.

I found a seat at a table in the back of the room and waited. The kid next to me introduced himself. He was named John Talbot, the third, but everybody called him Trey. "Get it?" he asked, smiling, just dying to explain to me. I didn't get it, not right away, but I said that I did.

Eventually a man with a crewcut came to a podium in the front of the room and started shuffling papers while a team of older boys—buttoned-down and khakied, combed and creased—distributed exam booklets and well-sharpened number two pencils with what seemed to me to be a slightly malicious, certainly self-satisfied composure.

No one is expected to know every answer, the instructions printed on the cover of the booklet read. The boys held the pencils out in a cigar box and let you select your own, like a dueling weapon. *Simply choose the most correct answer.* All those institutional pencils piled together like that gave me the willies. *Darken each circle completely.* I could feel my saliva starting to thicken, just like at the dentist's. I was going to get drilled.

Just then, as everyone was settling in and the proctor seemed ready to begin, I looked over my shoulder and spotted Mr. Walker, who was standing in the doorway. It was as if I had boarded the train, and having taken leave of me, he was still lingering on the platform. I felt like waving. He was looking right at me. And then—a little shyly at first, a little furtively—he started in. He touched his nose. He pulled his ear. He brushed his hand across the front of his shirt and tapped his forearm. It was a familiar series of gestures, a happy utterance in a private, unspoken language. It was the signal to hit away.

CHAPTER SEVENTEEN

As part of my application materials to the academy, I was supposed to submit a writing sample, an essay describing A Memorable Character. I put it off as long as possible, and then, lying on my bed with a notebook one Sunday night, I somehow got going on my father, just doodling with words, going nowhere in particular, and before I knew it, I had filled up five loose-leaf pages.

I didn't set out deliberately to lie or fabricate; my crime, such as it was, was not premeditated. It was like getting lost. I was going along fine and pretty soon I just wasn't telling the truth anymore—no more familiar markers in sight. I'd simply strayed. There was nothing really outrageous in it, no claims for heroism, no gross falsehoods, but neither was it true. I supplied some genuine particulars and invented a few more that suggested the kind of man any boy would be proud to claim as his father.

My father is a lawyer, I began. I described him as a man drawn to the practice of law by his strong sense of justice and fair play. I said that he worked *tirelessly*—it

was a word I loved, *tirelessly,* it was how Carl Yastrzemski was said to work in the cage in order to perfect
his swing, how Willie Mays shagged flies—on behalf of
his underdog clients, most recently a crippled farm boy.
I didn't mention anything about contingency fees or
his signature crying-on-demand summations or for that
matter, the fact that in regard to child support and a
judge's protection order, *he* was on the wrong side of
the law.

I constructed my own father from spare parts, like a
postmodern sculptor, glued together little scraps of
wood and wire, whatever was handy. I gave him a passionate nature, like Billy Martin; I gave him George
Walker's big hands. I even cribbed from my favorite
series of sports novels: Bronc Burnett's father had steely
gray eyes and a steady, rock-solid disposition, and,
now, so did mine. And just for the hell of it, I guess, I
gave him a sense of humor.

There was a certain amount of sentimental crap in it,
my dad playing catch with me, which really did happen,
but only once, a quick, impatient game years earlier, my
mother standing in the doorway supervising, something
sort of court-ordered about the whole thing, maybe a
half dozen throws in all, that ended—much to the relief
of both us—when a client called. I said that he delivered
groceries to his elderly mother and dropped hints about
various other, unspecified acts of generosity—I may not
have used the phrase "good deeds" but that was definitely my gist—which I could not describe with certainty, so private a man was he, practically secretive, so
little inclined to boast, but rather *suspected* him of.

I served him up, a manly stew, great chunks of decency and generosity in a rich bland broth. I typed a fair copy on my Brothers portable. When I finished, I read it over once more, more than a little pleased with myself, my way with words, a little proud of my father even, half convinced by my own language.

The next day, my mother took me by surprise. I'd just come home from school and was in the kitchen, rifling through cupboards, looking for something to eat. She was sitting at the table, smoking a cigarette and sipping a Tab. Without introduction, she launched into a reading of my essay. *My father is a lawyer.* I was squatting, staring at the canned goods, my back turned to her. It sounded familiar, but I couldn't place it right away. In her mouth, my words sounded different, hollow and unconvincing, like stiff lines from a bad play.

I turned around, a can of Campbell's vegetarian vegetable in hand. She reminded me of a newscaster reading a late-breaking bulletin—glasses on her nose, a handful of white paper, a certain seriousness of manner. The pop bottle in front of her could have been a microphone.

I sat down and waited. It went on and on, and my mother took her sweet time reading, giving every word its due weight. It was like being stopped at a train crossing watching an endless freight filled with my own bullshit roll slowly past. Finally, finally, she got to the end. My mother took her glasses off and looked at me.

"Steely gray eyes?" she said.

"Where'd you get that?" I said.

I'd left the essay on my desk, buried beneath of pile of sports magazines. My mother didn't go upstairs anymore. I knew my brother went through my things, but this was worse—now he was a jailhouse rat turning state's evidence.

"Steely gray eyes?" she said.

"I know it's garbage," I said. "I know it's a load of crap."

"This sounds like Jimmy Stewart," she said. *"Mr. Smith Goes to Law School.* Your father has green eyes."

"Come on," I said. "Who cares?"

"How about the time he flattened me in the living room," she said. "That was memorable, don't you think?"

I sat down and set the soup on the table. My mother leaned down and grabbed a fresh bottle of Tab from the eight pack on the floor next to her.

"And when he broke down the back door with a baseball bat," she said. "Wasn't that a time?"

"I'm sorry," I said.

She picked up a bent church key from the table and popped open her bottle. "Why'd you choose him?" she said.

"Who am I supposed to write about?" I said. "You?"

"You could do worse," she said.

"She drank Tab," I intoned, doing my best gravelly imitation of Walter Cronkite, *"lukewarm, right from the bottle,"* and then, pausing for effect, gave her back one of her own favorite, impressive-sounding words, *"in prodigious amounts."*

"How about this?" my mother said. *"She was a coura-geous, plucky woman, a pillar of strength to her sons, a real modern-day hero."*

I put my finger in my mouth and made a gagging sound.

"It's a stupid topic anyway," she said. "Hamlet is a character. Bullwinkle is a character. People aren't char-acters."

"It's just another test," I said. "A hoop you have to jump through."

"Well, you jumped through all right," she said. "Head first. Just like Sparky the seal. You deserve a piece of fish."

"You have to show them that you know how to play the game," I said.

"*You* have to," she said.

"As if you've never told a whopper," I said.

"Me?" she said.

"If I told the truth," I said, "they'd never accept me." As soon as I'd said that, I knew that I'd more or less put my finger on it.

My mother paused and lit a cigarette. "Look," she said. "I'm not saying it's bad because it's not true. It's bad because it's not that interesting."

"Okay," I said. "If you don't want me to use this, I won't."

I took the pages back. I wanted to put the damn thing in an envelope and seal it. I didn't want to look at what I'd written or hear it read again. I wanted to be done with it.

"Go ahead," she said. "I don't care. They'll probably

lap it up. Say something about his Purple Heart, mention the steel plate in his head. Do it up right. Put a little icing on the cake. Just don't you start to believe it, okay? That's all I'm saying."

I rolled the pages of my essay into a telescope and put it to my eye. I panned across the kitchen countertop, which was full of dirty dishes, empty bottles, a half-open jar of Skippy peanut butter.

"I don't blame you for lying," she said. "Drunks aren't that interesting. Some drink martinis, some drink Scotch. After a while, they all smell alike. Their livers turn to shoe leather. Eventually they're found dead in rented rooms."

While she talked, I turned my paper telescope on my mother and focused it right on her mouth. It was just like my old baseball card trick: one of those partial glimpses of a player Gerard and his friends tried to stump me with. I'd know my mother's mouth anywhere, but now, watching it in isolation, it surprised me a little. It was so full of muscular energy, it was like it had a life of its own. I wondered if her lips were numb. If they were, it didn't seem to matter. "Mouthy" was a favorite word of my mother's—applied always to my brother and me, a couple of mouthy kids—and it occurred to me that *she* was the mouthy one.

Her hand came up and she took a long drag from her cigarette, and I watched the ash glow red as she drew on it. She opened her mouth and let loose a great wave of white smoke, like something from a furnace.

"Your father used to be interesting, you know," she said.

"Really," I said. Watching her like that, I felt both present and safely distant, like I was off-camera, interviewing her. "Tell me something interesting about him," I said.

"Why he went to law school, for one thing," she said. "It wasn't because he loved truth and justice and the American way."

"Why then?"

"On a bet."

"A bet?" I said. I took the paper tube away from my eye.

"We were sitting in some pub downtown, your father and me and Charlie O'Connell," my mother said. "We'd been dating for a couple of months. Back then, your father had just gotten a job as a claims adjuster. He carried a clipboard. He inspected wrecked cars and burned-out buildings, assessed the damage. It was a step up from sweeping floors at Brown and Bigelow. Charlie, meanwhile, was in his first term at the St. Paul College of Law. He was absolutely full of himself. Charlie was the young John Marshall, the next Oliver Wendell Holmes, a little Felix Frankfurter. He spent most of the night going on and on about hard it was—all the reading and recitation, statutes and case law, torts and contracts—what a keen intellect it required. Now Charlie was a nice guy, but nobody ever accused him of having a keen intellect. I could see your father rattling his ice, getting impatient. 'I bet you couldn't hack it,' Charlie told him. And that was it. 'How much?' your father said. 'How much do you bet?' Charlie tried to weasel out of it, but eventually he named a price. I think it was a hundred dollars. They shook hands across the table, and the rest is history. Your father picked up an application the next morning. He'd been half tight, of course, and just trying to impress me, but it worked. I was impressed. And somehow I knew he would do it. And that I would marry him. I knew that, too. Back then, he had something that made you believe in him."

"Did he pay up?" I asked.

"Who?"

"Charlie O'Connell. Did he ever pay him the hundred bucks?"

"That's a good question," my mother said. "I don't rightly know. That's an excellent question."

I could see the wheels turning. She was probably thinking about compound interest, devising some quasi-legal argument to explain why the money rightly belonged to her. I knew she had Charlie O'Connell's number.

It was a good story, but I had no idea what it meant. I wasn't sure if I liked my father more or less for having become a lawyer in order to win a barroom bet. There were a lot worse, stupider reasons. In the end, I figured, it didn't really matter what I thought.

"So what else you want to know?" my mother asked.

"Does he really have a steel plate in his head?"

"What do you think?"

"It would explain some things," I said.

"Next time you see him," she said, "take a good look. Better yet, take a magnet to his scalp. He won't mind."

"Not much," I said.

. . .

That night, some time after midnight, my brother came into our room, smelling of beer and smoke, full of percussive anger. He rattled his keys and kicked off his shoes. He slammed a dresser drawer.

"Son of a bitch," he said.

He sat on the bed and lit a cigarette. "I hate this fucking place," he said. "I hate this room, I hate this house. I hate having to come home."

I lay there in the dark, motionless. I knew better than to engage him. He'd done it a few times before, come home and launched into a late-night rant. He complained about his harelipped boss, Mr. Kluge, whom he called Snuffy. Railed against his so-called friends. We both understood, I guess, that I was not expected to contribute. It was supposed to be a monologue. I just listened. It was a funny kind of intimacy, our last, I'm afraid. He would go on for a while, animated briefly by anger, running on rage fumes, but he couldn't sustain it. Pretty soon he'd slow down and then fall asleep. He'd done it before and he'd do it again.

"You're a good faker," Gerard said, "but you don't fool me. I know you're awake."

I could feel my heart beating, but I kept my eyes closed.

"You can fool some of the people some of the time," he said. "You can fool your baseball coach. Maybe you can fool the dickheads at the academy. But I've got news for you. You can't fool me."

I heard the bed creak then, and I knew Gerard was

lying down. I told myself to stay alert, to make sure that he didn't fall asleep with his cigarette burning. If there were flames, I decided, I could smother them with a blanket.

Suddenly there was a crack and I felt something, a sharp jab in the small of my back. It was my brother delivering a kick or a punch from down below.

"Who do you think you are?" he said. "Who the fuck do you think you are?"

He waited a moment, as if he expected me to answer.

He said, "You're a welfare boy, pal. That's what you are. A chickenshit, two-faced welfare boy. And your old man is a drunk. Face it. Your neat little essay and all your golden words aren't going to change that."

"You know what's wrong with you?" he said.

I waited for him to tell me. I was scared, but I was curious, too.

"You're just like him," Gerard said. "You're two peas in a fucking pod. A couple of smoothies. You're the Little Hawk. Junior. The heir fucking apparent."

Gerard's voice was starting to get quieter. He was losing steam. There wasn't much more he had to say. Before long, he'd be snoring.

In the morning, I'd get up and go about my business. I'd see my brother downstairs and we wouldn't talk about it. I'd imagine that he was sorry. In the light of day, I would understand that he didn't mean it, that his words didn't really apply to me.

CHAPTER EIGHTEEN

I spent the next Saturday afternoon working at Mr. Walker's. First, we cleaned his already spotless and pine-scented basement. It was unfinished—concrete floors and stone walls—but it was still brighter, more orderly, than our living quarters at home. There was a braided rug in front of the washer and dryer, a neat row of detergent bottles on a built-in shelf. There was a workbench, jars full of screws, saws and blades hanging from pegs on the wall. While Mr. Walker changed the filter in the furnace, I ran a broom over the floor.

Then we went upstairs and polished shoes. Mr. Walker conducted a little clinic for me, offered me instruction in the art of the shine. He had a wooden box, with a footrest built into the lid, full of paraphernalia: rags and brushes, cans of Kiwi polish, saddle soap and mink oil and paste wax, fresh packs of black and brown laces. We spread out newspapers on the kitchen floor and went to work. It was like something at the state fair, a hands-on demonstration.

I could dimly remember my mother, years earlier,

polishing my father's shoes the days he went to court. For her, it wasn't an educational opportunity, just a chore. But she did a good job, I seem to recall, with less equipment. Now, like it or not, I could almost hear her voice, could imagine the exact contours of her resent ment: I shined my share of shoes, she would say. Where'd it get me?

We practiced on a couple pairs of scuffed loafers Mr. Walker pulled from the front hall closet, jammed our hands in the shoes and brushed with long, loud strokes. At some point he really did spit, a bit of pure exuberant theatricality, I think, not strictly necessary, getting the job done with style, like Willie Mays making a basket catch. I don't know if many people even need to polish their shoes anymore—everything is specially treated now, all those miracle fabrics—but back then, to a guy like Mr. Walker, it meant something.

"Give them a good shine on Sunday night," Mr. Walker said. "Then touch 'em up mid-week. That's what I like to do."

It would have sounded corny if you tried to spell it out—self-respect, hard work, all those *Reader's Digest* values—but it was something real he wanted to give me.

"You know, the academy's headmaster is an old friend of mine," Mr. Walker said. "Wild Bill Kittle. That's what we called him. I don't even know why. He's actually not a bit wild. He's as tame as they come."

I smiled. An interviewer once asked the Mets' catcher Choo Choo Coleman how he got his nickname. I don't know, Choo Choo said. (When asked his wife's name, he supposedly responded, "Mrs. Coleman.")

"I'm going to drop him a line," Mr. Walker said. "Put in a good word for you. If you don't mind."

"I don't mind," I said.

"Not that you need it," he said.

What could I say? I was a polite kid; when Mr. Walker handed me a Coke, I said thank you. When he gave me five bucks for washing his car, I said thank you. But this time, it was different, my debt was quickly growing too vast even to acknowledge.

"Mr. Walker," I said.

"What?" he said.

"Thank you," I said.

"No problem," he said.

"I mean it," I said. "I really appreciate it."

"I know," he said. "I know you do."

"How come?" I asked him. "Why me?"

It was a stupid question, I realized as soon as I'd asked it. People don't know why they do what they do, even the good ones. Only a fool would ask.

Mr. Walker put his shoe down. His big hands were smudged with black polish. He looked at me, blinking, almost sad, and did his best. He told me that years ago, somebody had helped him out.

"Someday," he said, "you'll do the same. You'll help someone else out. It's just what people do."

I felt sorry for having put him on the spot. What gave me the right? I nodded and changed the subject.

Later, Mr. Walker went back upstairs and carried down more shoes, a whole cardboard carton full of them, some wing tips, a couple pairs of cleats, a pair of steel-toed work boots. We worked together for a long time,

and I didn't ask any more questions. We polished everything, and when we were done, I lined up Mr. Walker's
footgear along the wall in perfect, polished pairs.

I excused myself to go the bathroom, and when I
returned, I found Mr. Walker touching up a shoe I'd
already done. He looked embarrassed, but he didn't say
anything. He just kept working the brush back and
forth in a perfect, insistent machinelike rhythm.

My mother had promised to complete the academy's
required financial aid form, but she hadn't done it yet.
In Mr. Baumgarten's social studies class we'd studied
how a bill becomes law, and I knew all about the pocket
veto. The chief executive simply does nothing and that's
it. The legislation dies. In our textbook there was a cartoon drawing of a man slipping a sheet of paper in his
jacket pocket, a big self-satisfied smile on his face,
clearly pleased with himself and the cleverness of the
maneuver.

"Come on, Mom," I said. "It's already late."

She was sitting at the kitchen table, which was like
her office now, crowded with her stuff, whatever she
needed within easy reach—pens and paper, the telephone and coffeepot, her cigarettes and ashtray, a pack
of saltines and a jar of jam. A couple of times I'd found
her there asleep, head down, face flat against the tabletop, like a bored student snoozing in the back row. Her
bare feet were resting on a lumpy hassock she'd dragged
in from the living room. They were red and callused,
horribly swollen now, like something overly ripe, on the
verge of bursting.

"Okay," she said. "Okay. Let me see it."

I handed it over carefully. I didn't want it to get smeared with butter or stained with coffee, the way most of my homework papers did. She put her glasses on and looked it over, front and back. It was a simple form, a series of questions regarding the family's finances.

"Don't you think they'll wonder why your father, Mr. Memorable, won't be picking up this tab?"

"I haven't thought about it," I said, which was true.

"I'll have my accountant look this over and get back to you," she said.

"You promised," I said.

"Oh, all right," she said.

She picked up a felt-tip pen from the table and made some awkward, left-handed marks on the page, most of which seemed to be zeros, big fat defiant goose eggs. She squiggled something at the bottom—her signature, I assumed—and capped the pen with a flourish.

"There it is," she said. "Full disclosure. No runs, no hits, no assets."

I took it back and thanked her.

She lit a cigarette. "My pleasure," she said.

"You should go to the doctor," I said.

"Me?" she said. "Fit-as-a-fiddle me? Why should I go to a doctor?"

I motioned in the direction of the footstool. "Your feet," I said. I couldn't stand to look.

"You know what the trouble with doctors is?" she said.

The trouble with my mother was that she never gave

a straight answer—she danced, like Ali. I could never land anything. I just lumbered toward her, a big dumb clumsy load, like George Chuvallo.

"I give up," I said. "What's the trouble with doctors?"

"They don't give financial aid."

She picked up a deck of cards and started laying out a crooked game of solitaire. She played Vegas-style, once through the deck, five bucks for every card on the aces.

"When you go to the hospital," she said, "the first thing they want to know isn't where it hurts. It's *What's your insurance?* That's what they're interested in. You could be bleeding to death. No insurance, no doctor."

The cards were old, a grimy Hamm's Beer deck, but my mother made them snap somehow.

"So get some insurance," I said. "How much can it cost?"

"I made some calls," she said. "You know what I found out? I'm uninsurable. What do you think about that? If you don't need something, it's easy to get. But if you really need it, forget about it."

"That's stupid," I said. "It makes no sense."

"You can say that again," she said.

"That's stupid," I said. "It makes no sense."

"That's life," my mother said. "That's what all the people say."

She turned up the king of clubs, and I watched her slip it under the queen of hearts at the head of a column of cards.

"Hey," I said. "You can't do that. That's cheating."

"Who says?"

So I kept my mouth shut while she finished her game.

The next Saturday I was back at Mr. Walker's, helping him clean gutters. I held the ladder while he stood above me and dropped great globs of decomposed glop that exploded on the driveway like foul little bombs. I used Mr. Walker's big push broom to sweep the gunk into piles and then shoveled it into a can. Afterward he cleaned the driveway with the high-powered spray of his hose, square by square, until it was perfectly clean. To look at him—he was totally absorbed—you would have thought there was something more at stake than home maintenance, something life and death. When I made a joke about the driveway—if only I washed dishes so clean, I said, something like that—he half smiled, a little distractedly, as if he understood that it was funny, but only abstractly, in theory, the way a blind man grasps the idea of color.

After that we went inside for Cokes. We sipped and chatted, just like always. Somehow we got talking about the design of baseball mitts: the differences between infielders' and outfielders' gloves, the revolutionary hinged catcher's mitt, how the professional models were getting bigger and bigger every year. Mr. Walker told me that the glove he'd used when he pitched for the academy was tiny, a dinky piece of unpadded leather. "You'd be amazed," he said.

"I bet," I said.

He stood up. "It's in the attic," he said. "I know right where it is."

He headed upstairs, and I was alone in the kitchen. I glanced at a stack of mail on the kitchen counter—a telephone bill, something from a bank. I looked into the refrigerator. I'd done a little snooping around his house before—peeked into the medicine cabinet, opened a couple of closet doors—nothing too invasive. I was curious. I thought about him and his dead wife. He never talked about her, but I knew he missed her. Her name was Ann and she had shining black hair and loved roses. I wondered why there was no sign of her in the house. Had he thrown away her things? Sprayed them all away somehow? I thought there might be souvenirs hidden away somewhere, locked in a glass case, tokens and ticket stubs, the heart's collectibles. I think I wanted to see into his grief, find some evidence of it.

I opened one of the big oak cupboards. There were three or four tall boxes of Special K, a canister full of Lipton tea bags, two packages of English muffins, jars of orange marmalade all in a row. I felt a twinge of envy. He was a man who ate the same thing every morning. A man who never ran out. At the same time, though, I think I felt a kind of sad and dreary desperation in his order and routine, his clean gutters and sparkling driveway. I knew what Special K tasted like.

At the end of the counter, next to Mr. Walker's toaster, I noticed a folded piece of paper tucked inside a napkin holder. It was a letter, addressed to the academy's headmaster, a draft, I suppose—typed with a few marginal corrections made in Mr. Walker's characteristically neat hand. I could hear him moving around in the attic, his footsteps, while I read:

Dear Bill,

I am writing on behalf of Harlan Hawkins in hopes that you'll give him special consideration, not just for admission for next year's freshman class but also for financial aid.

As his summer baseball coach and neighbor, I can say that he is a good boy. Though blessed with only modest athletic ability, he's made the most of his talent. He is a smart player, a student of the game. I've hired him to do odd jobs for me, and found him to be hard-working and reliable. I never have to tell him something twice. He is quiet, a little shy, but always attentive and respectful.

You'll see that his academic record is strong. His grades are excellent, he's at the very top of his class. But what his transcript won't show is that he's done this well in spite of the fact that he comes from a broken home and a very troubled family situation. His father is an attorney, a brilliant man, I am told, but sadly, he has a drinking problem. The mother is an invalid whose condition, I believe, is deteriorating. They are recently divorced. Their home life, I'm afraid, is chaotic.

In the right environment, with the right sort of guidance, I believe Harlan Hawkins will flourish. But he needs the stability and structure and the role models you can offer. We both know that the academy has a justified reputation for opening its doors to underprivileged boys. I hope you'll keep the tradition alive and give this fine young man a chance to succeed. He won't disappoint.

Yours most sincerely,
George Walker

I heard Mr. Walker on the stairs and slid the letter back in the holder. I felt wobbly. It wasn't just the disconcerting effect of reading about myself over someone's shoulder, in the third person. Modest athletic ability didn't bother me. Fair enough. I liked being called a student of the game. It was something else.

CHAPTER NINETEEN

In our house, the mail slot emptied directly into the back of the hall closet, so that whatever our carrier dropped in would often disappear amid all the stuff already crammed in there: grocery bags full of family photographs, Christmas decorations, board games, school papers, baseballs and gloves, skates and sticks and pucks, a thigh-high pile of winter coats and hats and boots from over the years, layered like archeological deposits. My brother and mother didn't pay much attention to the mail, they let me take care of it. I may have been the only one nimble and determined enough to retrieve it.

Having completed my application to the academy, I checked the mail more and more often, sometimes a couple of times a day, looking for some official word of acceptance. I wanted some good news. Besides, I sort of liked digging around back there. When I could think of nothing else to do, I'd spend some time rummaging around in that closet, seeing what I could turn up. I could have dragged what I wanted into the living room

and looked at it there, but I must have liked the privacy
and safety of that small space. Sometimes I'd find something good—a decent catalog, free samples of something
edible—sometimes not. It was hit or miss, like fishing or
panning for gold, domestic archival research, mildly
purposeful boredom with an edge of anticipation.

More and more, I spent time in that closet just looking at old photographs. They'd been there for years but
I found myself newly drawn to them. There was one
picture of Gerard I used to look at again and again. He
was no more than two, maybe three years old. It was a
studio portrait: He was in front of a blue backdrop, his
hair damp and combed to a little bump in the front, a
big, delighted smile on his face. Whatever happened to
him hadn't happened yet. That's the only way I can
describe it. It wasn't just that he hadn't yet gotten fat,
though that was part of it, I suppose. There was something about him, a kind of sheen, that had been rubbed
off or worn away before I'd even got to know him. In
this photograph, his eyes were so blue I thought at first
they must have been retouched somehow. It was heart-
breaking. I felt tremendous uncomplicated affection for
this bright-eyed boy. He was my dead brother, the one I
would never get to know, and I used to wonder what
suffering he had had to endure.

There was a whole batch of black-and-white pictures
of my mother trying to look like a movie star or a pinup
girl—her hair done up, wearing a black bathing suit that
showed off her long smooth legs and delicate ankles.
Even though she was my mother, I could see that she
was good-looking. Now her feet were constantly

swollen, cracked and callused, her legs stiff and recalcitrant. But I could still remember our foot races across
Harmon Field to the car after my little league games,
and back then, my mother, who never let me win, not at
checkers, not at anything, was fast—she beat me every
time.

One day I found a thick folder of materials from a
night-school course she must have taken before she got
married. It was some kind of vocabulary-building class.
There were long lists of alphabetized words, arranged in
numbered units: *parsimonious, portentous, pretentious,
prodigious.* She'd aced nearly every quiz as far as I
could tell, always circled the correct choice: *maladroit,
malfeasance, malleable.* So many of these were what I
thought of as uniquely my mother's words, words she
still used, savored, picked up and brandished in argu-
ments like a favorite glittering letter opener. Churlish
and cretinous, egregious and equivocate. Even though I
knew these words were in the public domain, I thought
of some of them as her personal possessions. I didn't
believe I'd ever heard another person use them. I felt
half embarrassed to have stumbled upon these, as if I'd
discovered a secret I shouldn't have been permitted to
know. It was weird. Even though I probably would
have looked at anything of hers I could have gotten my
hands on—a diary, love letters, you name it—these lists
seemed even more personal somehow.

The only photograph of my father I could ever find
was a picture postcard that he must have had taken of
himself on a business trip: GREETINGS FROM THE WINDY
CITY. He was standing in front of a brick building with a

sport coat draped over his shoulder. Just like my father to think he was the most interesting sight in Chicago.

Best of all, I think, I liked the snapshots taken in our house on birthdays and holidays. I loved looking at the household scenery: the oversized balloons hanging from the light fixture in the dining room, the elaborate centerpieces, the table set with goblets and the apple-patterned dishes we'd long ago either broken or stowed away. It was always my mother who aimed the camera, so I could tell what caught her eye, what she must have been proud of—a vase of fresh-cut flowers, holly and pine boughs fashioned into a wreath. I felt glad that our family had once seemed to have enjoyed a kind of golden age, a time of tablecloths and candles, a time when our carpet, now frayed and worn to the backing in some spots, looked thick and new. And I was glad that there was a record of it that I could consult whenever I wanted.

One day I found an envelope with a February postmark on the floor of that closet with my name on it. It was from Nana—I recognized her return address. There was a letter inside, a half-sheet of stationery filled with faint, feathery handwriting, her lines so tremulous they looked ornate, each letter decorated with impossibly small flourishes and curlicues.

It was a pleasure, my grandmother wrote, to have seen me again. Her words on the page looked to me exactly the way her voice sounded—formal, a little faint. I could practically hear her. She hoped to see me more often, to become better acquainted. Reading about baseball, she said, had helped to entertain the irksome hours, and she looked forward to further discussions with me. In the meantime, she had some questions, some terms she'd like me to explain: suicide squeeze, slugging percentage, Baltimore chop, the old pepper game. Enclosed was a newspaper clipping, from the *New York Times* travel section, I believe, about Cooperstown, New York.

Nana had been a teacher for many years, and now, it was as if she were giving me an assignment, signing me up as her pupil in some kind of correspondence course. I'd always liked school, and could imagine becoming a teacher myself. I liked the prospect of a new roster of hopeful talent every September, just like spring training, the season of optimism, all possibility and potential. I wondered what kind of teacher Nana had been. I could almost see her standing at the head of a scrubbed and earnest class, fiery and demanding, a kind of schoolroom Eddie Stanky brandishing a pointer. I wondered what kind of mother she had been, too. She'd had two boys, just like my mother. One killed himself, and one grew up to be my father.

"Nana is a baseball fan," I told my mother.

"Since when?" my mother said. She had the Sunday newspaper spread out in front of her on the kitchen table, a Styrofoam cup of coffee at her elbow, a cigarette in hand.

"She reads the sports page," I said. "She studies the box scores."

"She reads everything," my mother said. "She studies everything. The comics, the weather map. She studies the obituaries. What kind of fan does that make her?"

"Gerard thinks she's rich," I said. She had thousands socked away in the stock market, he told me, shares in Ford, Coca-Cola, GE.

"Gerard wishes she's rich," she said.

"Oh," I said, noncommittal.

"Don't get your hopes up," she said. "That woman would steal the pennies off a dead man's eyes. If she does have a bundle sewed into her mattress, she's going to take it with her, I swear. She's going to find a way to do it."

"How come you don't like her?"

"She lost interest in me when I kept flunking her tests," my mother said.

"What tests?"

"Fill-in-the-blank Shakespeare," my mother said. " 'Now what's the next line, dear,' she would say. 'It escapes me. Do you recall?' No, I don't recall, I told her. I never knew so I guess I can't recall. So forget it, I told her. Call off the oral exam. I'll be damned if I was going to be quizzed by my mother-in-law."

"I know about Dad's brother," I said. "I know it wasn't a car accident."

She didn't look surprised, just curious.

"Why did he do it?"

My mother took one last drag on her cigarette and

dropped her butt in the dregs of her coffee. "Why do you think?" she said.

"I don't know," I said.

"I don't know, either," she said. "He was just a kid. Nobody knows. He must have given up. He probably felt like he couldn't take another step. He probably felt hopeless."

She rubbed the back of her neck, hard, kneading it, like the beginnings of a self-administered massage. "You ever feel that way?" she said.

"Maybe," I said.

"Well, maybe I do, too," she said. "Maybe everybody does sometimes."

"Sure," I said.

"You know what to do then?" she said. "When you feel like giving up?"

"What?" I said. "Tell me."

"Don't," she said.

I thought about paying Nana a visit after that, but I never did. My plan was to stop first at the grocery store to pick up some Fig Newtons, maybe a couple cans of creamed corn, and then take the bus over to her house. I knew which line, which stop exactly, where I'd have to yank the cord. It would make her day. We'd sit in the kitchen and talk baseball. I'd not only explain the squeeze play, I'd stand up and demonstrate, show her how it's done. And having come up with the plan, especially one so detailed, I felt pretty good about myself, almost as if I'd actually done it.

· · ·

Finally, on a chilly April afternoon, I found my letter from the academy. I stood up in the closet, knee-deep in junk, and held it up to the light. I could see that the message it contained was short, which I knew was good. *I am pleased to inform you*, it began. That's all I remember. It was a form letter on bond paper. William Kittle, Mr. Walker's friend, the headmaster, had scrawled his name at the bottom, a couple of hurried loops in blue ink. Somehow, after weeks of anticipation, the thing itself was a disappointment. It was not what I had imagined, though I couldn't say what it was that I had been imagining. Just not this.

When I showed the letter to my mother, she didn't seem especially interested. She was sitting at the kitchen table, her usual spot, paging through cookbooks, a new diversion. Now that she'd apparently lost much of her taste for food, she seemed to enjoy reading about it, looking at pictures of it. Her favorites were oversize, illustrated volumes from the fifties, probably wedding presents, full of photographs of happy homemakers and their meat-eating hubbies.

"I'm in," I told her. "I got my acceptance."

"Congratulations." She barely looked up from Betty Crocker's red-and-white, ring-bound picture cookbook. "Your dream come true," she said, which may have been either a statement or a question, I wasn't sure.

I put the letter in front of her, hoping she would read it, but she pushed it aside. "You don't have to prove anything to me," she said.

"It's hard to believe," I said. In less than a year, it occurred to me, I might be sitting at the table in my blue uniform. Maybe by then I would know how to tie a tie.

"Here's a recipe for 'emergency steak,' " my mother said. "I like the sound of that, don't you?"

"Sure," I said.

We were alike. My mother had her cookbooks. I had my baseball cards, my academy brochures, Mr. Walker's yearbooks, those sweet-smelling textbooks. All that glossy perfection. One crippled, one scrawny, the two of us in our grimy kitchen, dreaming.

"Or how about this," she said. She turned the book toward me, held it open like a first-grade teacher reading to her class. " 'Homefront macaroni.' Doesn't that look good?"

I had to admit it, yes, it looked good.

"What do you think it tastes like?"

CHAPTER TWENTY

The next night, sometime before midnight, when I was lying in bed but hadn't yet fallen asleep, I heard some rumbling on the street and the thud of a car door. I looked out my bedroom window and saw a yellow cab at the curb. I thought, bingo, another check, and by the time I had clattered down the stairs to the front door, I already had a good chunk of it spent: a decent television, for one thing—color would be nice, but anything with a real antenna and a full set of knobs would do—I was sick of looking at ghosts. A new first baseman's mitt for me. A couple of cases of Tab and a visit to the doctor for my mother—cash and carry, who needs insurance when you have a wad of bills? That's what I figured. Problem solved.

I fumbled with the lock for a moment—you had to jiggle it, give it some shoulder, turn and push at the same time, like an aspirin bottle cap—and when I finally got the door open, I saw the cabby standing on the front porch with his back turned, his head bent, massaging his temples. There was a shoe box–sized package tucked under one arm. He was a worn, tired-looking guy in his shirtsleeves. He looked to me like he was at the end of his shift. Except it wasn't a cabby. It was my father.

"Dad?" I said.

He turned slowly to face me and with a flourish, tipped an invisible hat in my direction. His face was glazed and swollen-looking, pouched and punched, like a weary, badly beaten heavyweight. The front of his white shirt was splashed with dark stains—blood, steak sauce, who knows what. He smiled then, quick and phony, a little angry even, a photo-op smile.

"C'est moi," he said.

"Dad," I said.

I felt like crying, I don't know why. Compared to my outsize recent memories of him—murderously battering our back door; shaking his dice cup and calling for another round, all that barroom bluster and bullshit; standing in his camel coat outside the liquor store and coolly lighting a smoke—he seemed sadly pale and shrunken. He didn't look like a memorable character at all. Part of me would have rather seen him snarl than smile like that.

He said, "Happy birthday, Sport."

My birthday wasn't for another three weeks, but I wasn't about to say anything. He was close anyway, I figured, he had the month right. He deserved partial credit.

"Thanks," I said.

He stepped forward and pushed the package into my hands. It was wrapped in brown paper, an inside-out grocery bag maybe, lots of tape, no card, no tag. "Go ahead," he said. "Open it."

He put a cigarette between his lips and started patting his pockets, searching for something to light it with, while I tore off the paper. Inside was a gray box with some printing on the side: 25% COTTON FIBER, 500 COUNT. I lifted the lid and pulled out something wrapped in tissue paper.

It was a little trophy. There was a small golden man standing on the top of a Dixie cup–sized cylinder, not looking especially athletic, a nondescript, featureless figure with his arms at his side and a billed cap on his head. He looked like a fisherman whose pole had been snapped off—he had that bland and patient air about him. At the base there was a glued-on plate with an inscription: "THE GREATEST." I remember thinking it was funny that there was no noun. The greatest what? I wondered. Plus it was in quotation marks: the so-called greatest.

With that trophy in hand, I felt like I should make a speech. But I couldn't think of anything to say. "Thanks," I said.

"Well deserved," my father said. He was going through his pockets again, still looking for a match.

There were other things in the box. I reached in and took out another tissue-wrapped bundle—a big black-faced Bulova watch with a heavy gold band. It wasn't new—the crystal was scratched, and the next day I would discover an engraved inscription on the back: LOVE, NANCE—but it was still impressive. The only watch I'd ever owned was my first-communion Timex. I slipped it on and we watched it roll around my wrist.

"They can just take a link out," my father said.

"Maybe a couple," I said.

"No problem," he said.

At the bottom of the box there were some books, three crackling old leather-bound volumes: *The Meditations of Marcus Aurelius, The Call of the Wild,* an anthology of English Romantic poetry. I lifted them out one at a time, as gently as I could.

"When I was your age," my father said, "those books were my guides. They were shining lights in a dark world."

"Really," I said. I wasn't sure if he was pulling my leg or not. With him, I was never sure.

I opened the poetry book and leafed through it. The pages were delicate, tissue-thin—it was Bible paper. There were passages underscored in pencil, and faint, feathery annotations in the margin, which I recognized immediately as Nana's. Her commentary looked mostly earnest and appreciative, lots of exclamations: *Beautiful!* she'd written at the bottom of "To a Skylark," her letters so light they looked hushed—it was what a whisper looks like. And next to the last stanza of Keats's "Ode on Melancholy" she'd penciled in *lovely, sad, so true.*

"Listen to this," my father said. He cleared his throat and closed his eyes:

> *Like one, that on a lonesome road*
> *Doth walk in fear and dread,*
> *And having once turned round walks on,*
> *And turns no more his head;*
> *Because he knows, a frightful fiend*
> *Doth close behind him tread.*

"Not bad?" he said, clearly proud of himself. There was a kind of Barrymore bombast in his delivery, but I liked it. It was dramatic, atmospheric nonsense, harmless hot air. When he was a kid, Nana used to pay him for memorizing verse, that's what my mother told me. A penny a poem, something like that.

"Classics," my father said. "These are classics."

With his pointless poetry and grab bag full of pawnshop gifts, my father reminded me of the Wizard of Oz, exposed—a humbug, Dorothy calls him. My father was a humbug.

"At the academy," my father said, "they're gonna expect that you know the classics."

"You know about that?" I said. "The academy?"

"You'd be surprised what I know."

"Who told you?"

"Reliable sources," he said.

His buddy Tony Becker liked to use headers like that in his column: DON'T PRINT THAT, HEARD IT HERE FIRST, RELIABLE SOURCES. It never amounted to much—somebody's sore hamstring, a locker room scuffle, trade rumors—but it didn't matter; guys like Becker and my father must have loved the inside sound of it, the scoop and the skinny, the clear dope.

"After that, pal, the sky's the limit," he said. "The Ivy League. A crimson *H* on your jacket. You can write your own ticket."

So that explains it, I figured. This sudden interest. If I went to a fancy school, it would give him something to brag about, just like my phantom no-hitters.

"Do me proud," he said. "That's all I ask. I know you will."

He gave a little cough and wiped an eye with the back of his hand. I think he was actually tearing up a little, starting to choke with what he must have thought was fatherly feeling. There was a great undigested lump of emotion stuck in his throat. Drunk or sober, genuine, fake, or manufactured—I don't think he knew the difference anymore. A farm boy with no legs. His kid headed off to school. I could remember him coming home years earlier, red-eyed and sniffling, full of soggy sorrow, crying because Herbert Hoover had died. Herbert Hoover!

I heard a noise behind me then—something mechanical, something human, a creak and a groan—and my father looked up. It was my mother stepping slowly out, holding onto the door with one hand for balance, her bad foot dragging behind.

"Here comes trouble," my father said.

She was holding a big kitchen knife in her hand. I knew for a fact that it was dull as could be—it was her all-purpose knife, what she hacked and whacked and jimmied things with around the house. But even so. It was a big knife, it made an impression.

She looked like someone who meant business.

"Trouble?" she said. "You want trouble? I'll give you trouble."

My father raised his hands to his shoulders and held them there, palms up. "No thank you," he said. "I surrender."

"Just like always," my mother said. "Surrender was always your style. You always excelled at surrender."

"I'm a lover," he said. "Not a fighter."

She pointed the knife at him. "Don't get cute," she said.

"Oh, come on," he said. "Would you really? In cold blood? In front of the child?"

"With pleasure," she said.

"Go ahead then," he said. He lowered his hands and stood there, an unlit Camel dangling from his lip, a man in a stained shirt awaiting the fatal blow.

It was the stuff of melodrama, sure, a performance, I understood, at least partly for my benefit. I was like an extra with a nonspeaking part, a guy holding a flag at the back of the stage, a marginal player, but I was a member of the audience, too—my presence seemed necessary somehow. Maybe my being there juiced things up a little, inspired them to bring something—some new passion or conviction or meaning—to their tired old feud.

"This will be considered premeditated," he said. "You're looking at life without parole. Just so you know."

"What's the difference?" she said. "I'm looking at life without parole now."

Across the street, lights were going on in Mrs. Gunsher's house, upstairs, downstairs, her porch light, the floodlight in the back, the works.

My father shifted his feet a little. "All right then," he said. "Suit yourself. Stick it to me. Bury the dagger. Put me out of my misery once and for all."

My mother took a half step forward and pushed the knife toward his gut. For a split second, I thought this had suddenly gone way beyond play-acting, I thought my mother had gone nuts—I thought she was going to stab him. My father must have thought so, too. He hadn't really moved—his hands were still raised, his feet planted—but his eyes were wide and white.

"You're scared," my mother said. She was right in his face now, like a feisty D.I. "You're a coward," she said.

"Yes," my father said. "Absolutely."

"And you look like hell," my mother said. The way she said it, it wasn't an accusation, just the sad truth.

"I myself am hell," he said.

"You said it," my mother said, and lowered her knife.

My father's face relaxed a little. To me, he looked—I don't know how else to say it—reprieved.

"You hit that particular nail squarely on the head," she said.

"You got a light?" he asked.

My mother reached into a pocket and took out a plastic lighter. She flicked it a couple of times and finally brought forth a small flame. She extended it toward my father and he bent his head over the flame and inhaled.

In that gesture, there was something tender and familiar, a kind of practiced intimacy—they'd so obviously been married. It's an image I've carried around with me for years: the two of them, standing side by side, crippled and drunk, stained and disheveled, my mother's hand, my father's face, a weak flame.

My father straightened up and took a long drag. My mother pocketed her lighter and rested a hand on my father's elbow. I had a vivid memory of them years earlier, getting ready to go out on a Saturday night—my mother wearing pearls and making lipstick faces in the mirror, my father in a sleeveless undershirt, smelling of shaving cream, standing at her side, watching. He sticks two cigarettes in his mouth, lights them both, and hands one off to her. Back then, they seemed glamorous to me and their wordless affection was unfathomable but real, like gravity. Then something happened. Now they were a couple of people whose lives had become a loud, unlucky mess. It happens. They weren't evil, I told myself. They were just not very good at being adults is all.

"Do you want some coffee?" my mother said.

"Nah," my father said.

It must have been Mrs. Gunsher across the street who called the police. I suppose she'd been watching out the front window, her binoculars pressed to her face. Maybe that little business with the knife scared her. In any case, a squad car pulled up then, lights flashing, but no siren, with two officers inside. They stayed in the car for what felt like an awfully long time.

We stood there on the front steps, my parents and I, watching and waiting. The driver flicked on the overhead light and wrote something on a clipboard. Nobody said anything. Finally, they got out, stiff and slow, like two guys on a long car trip, and made their way up the front walk. I recognized one of them—he'd come to the house back in June when my father had fallen asleep in the hammock. This fellow—Malucci, his shirt said—led the way up the front walk with his partner trailing behind.

"Evening folks," he said. "How we doing?"

"*We're* doing fine," my mother said.

The two of them, Malucci and his partner, did this thing that cops do—they must teach it at the academy—took my parents apart, my father on one side of the lawn, my mother on the other side, separated by some safe distance, and let them talk. The cop stands there, physically present but staring off, toeing the dirt, like a manager making a pitching change, big and bland, absorbing bile, betrayal, outrage, jealousy—all thirty-one flavors of domestic disturbance—like bread sopping up gravy, like some sort of human antacid.

I stayed on the steps and watched them work. West St. Paul cops wore olive green uniforms—pale, pocketed dress shirts, dark pants with a thick black stripe on the side, matching Ike jackets—which made them look like bus drivers. It didn't really matter, I guess, cops were cops—we used to call any umpire "Blue," even if it was just a guy in street clothes. There wasn't much serious crime on their turf, no murder, no rape, no assault or armed robbery; the police blotter in the local weekly was full of cracked windshields and DWIs, lost children, a few domestic disturbances. These guys were perfect, got the job done with their umpire's, their bus driver's virtues—they showed up on time, knew the rules, stayed calm, and kept things from getting out of hand.

Malucci took my father, who gesticulated and ranted, but not too much, less than I expected. He said something about Miranda and unlawful detainment, talking about his constitutional rights as if they were exclusively his, his and his alone. All the while he was cutting the air with his right arm, winding up—my father was the Satchel Paige of rhetorical gesture, an old-fashioned double-pumper—and pointing at poor Malucci, part accusation, part emphasis, his own physical italics, shaking his balled fist back and forth as if he were sprinkling him with liquid contempt from some invisible dispenser. He fumed and sputtered but he kept his hands to himself. My father seemed to understand that cops were just like umpires: You could holler and point at them all you want, you could even spit and kick dirt in their general direction. But it's not okay to touch them, and there are some words you can't say.

My mother talked to the other cop—Hairston, his name was. "That woman across the street," she said, "she calls an awful lot doesn't she? I know she's a regular. Two, three times a week? She's thinks the neighborhood is full of suspicious characters, prowlers and peeping Toms. Now tell me honestly, Mr. Hairston, what Tom in his right mind would want to peep at her?

"Isabel Gunsher," my mother said. "She lives all alone in that big house, breathing stale air and dust, surrounded by her doilies and waxed fruit and crucifixes and photographs of the late lamented Mr. Gunsher, living on prune juice and tuna fish. Listening to *Dialing for Dollars*. Her eyes are bothering her. She's blind in one eye and has cataracts in the other. It's a sad life, don't you think?"

Hairston fiddled uneasily with his big gold class ring. He didn't look at all like a serious law enforcement officer. He was awfully young, for one thing. He had acne. There was an NBA player named Hairston, nicknamed Happy, a hard-rebounding forward for the Pistons. This fellow didn't look happy. He looked dumb and self-conscious, like a slow student in a spelling bee, just waiting for his humiliation to pass so he could get it over with and sit down.

"Yes, ma'am," he said.

"Of course it is," my mother said.

Mrs. Gunsher was standing in her picture window. The lights were on behind her; we could see her in perfect scrawny, scared silhouette. My mother gave a big energetic, sweeping overhand wave, the way you'd signal an airplane.

"Busybody bitch," she said. "Nosy Parker."

Nobody paid any attention to me. I sat down on the step and waited. I fooled with my new watch a little. On my wrist, it looked ridiculous, less like jewelry than armor, like something Hercules wore. I watched the sweep of the second hand and timed my parents: It was twenty seconds before I saw my father pause to take a breath, it took my mother just under two minutes to finish her cigarette.

What a phrase like "domestic disturbance" can never convey is the boredom, what a slow and grinding game it is. I felt like I was one of the ball club's extra men, sitting in the dugout, watching the action on the field. You had to stay loose, just in case.

That's when I spotted Mr. Walker, half a block down the sidewalk, headed our way. He was walking with a sort of mild purpose, less urgent than exercise, swifter than a nature walk, more like he was headed to the store to buy something inessential. He was wearing khakis and a windbreaker. He slowed as he approached our house, taking it all in, I'm sure—the squad car, the cops, my father and mother haranguing them—doing a quick damage assessment maybe—no blood, no broken glass. Not this time anyway.

I stood up. "Mr. Walker," I said. He came over and shook my hand. Under the circumstances it was a strangely formal gesture, but it felt right somehow, equal parts greeting and condolence and reassurance. He held on longer than a handshake, strictly speaking, dictated, but that was fine, I didn't mind. His right hand wasn't just huge, it was warm, too. That was the condolence, a little bit of human heat. We'd shaken hands when he'd lost his wife, and now we were shaking again.

"You're okay?" he said.

"I'm okay," I said.

"Sure?" he said.

"I'm sure," I said.

"Excuse me for just a minute," he said. "I'll be right back."

Mr. Walker drifted over to where my father and Malucci were standing, and then, like a skilled cocktail party mingler, insinuated himself into their conversation, such as it was. My father was still talking, more quietly now, but insistently. If he was surprised to see Mr. Walker, he didn't let on. He just nodded and became a bit more animated, playing to his new audience.

"A man brings his son a birthday present," he said. "Is that against the law?" He turned toward Mr. Walker now, appealing to him—at last, a jury—"I ask you, is that a crime? Loving your son? Then I am guilty. Guilty as charged."

It was damn strange to see them together, Mr. Walker and my father. Of course they knew each other—they'd been neighbors for years, they must have passed each other on the street, waved and made remarks about the weather or something. But let's face it, my father was no backyard barbecuer, no trimmer of hedges, no washer of cars. I'd never seen him wear short pants, not once. He didn't do lawn and garden. He argued and orated, declaimed and recited, he speechified and swore, but he didn't chat. I couldn't call up a single, specific memory of seeing Mr. Walker and my father together.

My mother, meanwhile, was still banging Hairston's ears about something. I couldn't quite make out the words, but I heard her voice, adding the high harmony to my father's song of complaint, grievance, and self-pity.

Very briefly I entertained a fantasy of Mr. Walker chewing my parents out, grabbing them by the scruffs of their stupid necks, like a teacher breaking up a play-ground brawl, forcing sweaty and tear-stained them to shake hands, work it out, *get over it,* right now, before the bell rings, while he looked on, the owlish, strong-handed embodiment of good sense and fair play. But I knew better. Intervention was not Mr. Walker's style, yelling and head-banging was not his style. He walked softly and carried a fungo bat, which he would never raise in malice. He was the quiet voice of reason, he was Woodrow Wilson, he was the League of Nations.

. . .

Finally, after about five more minutes or so of standing around and a short conference of the cops, Malucci steered my father over to the squad car. That's how it all played out. He didn't protest, he didn't complain. At some point I think he may have realized he was going to need a ride. I don't think they actually arrested him—they could have, I suppose, he was drunk, if not disorderly—but they did take him away.

We stood there and watched, my mother, Mr. Walker, and I, while Hairston held the door, like a valet, and my father got into the car slowly, with a kind of injured dignity. Slumped in the backseat, he looked vaguely felonious, discredited, almost stately somehow, but soiled and shadowy.

My mother had told me that he was going to be found dead in a rented room, and I didn't doubt her. I don't suppose he deserved it, but I felt sorry for him anyway. Right then I felt sorry for everybody—my father and mother, my brother and me, too, Tony Becker and his reliable sources, Mrs. Gunsher, Malucci and his pimply-faced partner, Unhappy Hairston, who did this every day, Herbert Hoover, the whole sorry sad lot of us.

CHAPTER TWENTY-ONE

She was sitting at the kitchen table shuffling her grimy Hamm's Beer cards. There was a picture-postcard photograph of a cool blue lake reproduced on the backs along with their slogan in bright red script: FROM THE LAND OF SKY BLUE WATERS.

"Mom," I said, and sat down across from her. It had been a week since my father's last late-night visit.

She held the deck toward me in her left hand, her thumb and fingers placed precisely along its edges, then carefully let half the cards drop into her palm, and with two quick movements, executed a neat one-hand cut.

"Hey," I said. "Can you teach me how to do that?"

"No," she said.

"No?"

"Some things," she said, "you have to learn by yourself."

She put the deck down in front of her on the table, where she'd pushed aside the tabletop clutter—newspapers and dirty dishes, her cigarettes and lighter, empty pop bottles and condiments, ashtrays and aspirin—to create a free space the size of a place mat, like a small clearing in a thick forest. She started turning cards over one at a time, studying each one, slowly lining them up on the table, some face up, some face down, in what I imagined was some crazy new crossword-style variation of solitaire.

"I'm not going to the academy," I said. "I don't care how much aid they give me, I don't want to go."

I'm not sure exactly when I'd made up my mind, but I had. Reading Mr. Walker's letter had something to do with it. Talking to my father had something to do with it, too. But there was no list of pros and cons; no one thing was decisive. It didn't even feel like I was deciding so much as admitting, saying some true things out loud. There was a reason that even in my imagination I could not insinuate myself into the shining academy world: I could picture the grounds and classrooms and playing fields, but not myself among them. I didn't want to be anybody's project. I didn't want to do my father proud. I was never going to be friends with some pricks in button-downs with Roman numerals after their names. If my home was broken, so be it.

"I'm not surprised," she said.

"What do you mean?" I said.

I guess I'd fancied myself something of a dark horse. The prospect of catching her flat-footed, of landing at least one roundhouse, had appealed to me. I'd wanted her to be surprised.

"I know you," she said. She pointed to the red jack she'd just turned over. "I know your heart," she said.

"I'll probably regret it," I said. "I'm probably making a big mistake."

"I certainly hope so," she said. "Why make a small mistake? I mean, why bother? Forget the nickel-and-dime stuff. Swing away. If you're going to go wrong, do it in a big way, that's what I always say."

"Thanks," I said. "Thanks a lot."

"A little regret is a good thing," she said. "Take it from an expert." She glanced across the table. "It's the spice of life," she said. "It's cayenne pepper. It's garlic."

She reached over and picked up a bottle of Tabasco. "Regret," she said. "It's hot sauce in the great stew of life. It stings a little, but it keeps things interesting. When you burn your tongue, you know you're alive. It cleans out your system. It's Coca-Cola in your carburetor. After a while, you get used to it."

She unscrewed the bottle cap and shook a couple of red drops onto her finger and licked it.

"And then," she said, "you learn to love it."

"How about a lot of regret?" I said. "Is that a good thing?"

She pushed the Tabasco bottle across the table at me. "Help yourself," she said.

"No thanks," I said. "Not before five o'clock."

"I'm sorry," she said. "Did you think your little life was going to be a perfect game? Three up and three down, inning after inning? There's nothing more boring than goose eggs. I thought you'd have figured that out by now."

Mr. Walker had called her an invalid, which I knew she was, but, I believed, only in some technical, letter-of-recommendation sense, in exactly the same sense that I was underprivileged and deserving. (I'd gone so far as to look up "invalid" in the dictionary: a chronically ill or disabled person.) It was the kind of vocabulary you used to turn misery into cash—I'd heard it on *Queen for a Day,* read it at Christmastime in the Neediest Fund. It was a kind of box to check. A way to cut to the front of the line. But a word like that mattered to me, I don't know why, and once I'd read it, I couldn't forget about it. My idea of an invalid was sort of doughy and stationary, helplessly good and desperately nice, a rosary in one hand, a blanket on the lap, a grateful piece of human furniture to be lugged around. Not someone who considered Tabasco sauce a beverage.

"I'm worried about Mr. Walker," I said. "I'm afraid he's going to be disappointed."

"He might be," she said. "A little. Maybe a little relieved, too."

My mother turned over the king of spades. She made a little sound, distress or pleasure, I couldn't tell. She placed it on top of the king of diamonds and turned them both over.

"Are there rules?" I asked.

"Rules?" she said.

"In your game," I said.

"This is a game?" she said. "Is that what you think?"

"Then what is it?"

She took a cigarette from her pack on the table, put in it her mouth, and lit it with her plastic lighter. She took a long drag and blew out a couple of wobbly rings. "Divination," she said.

"Divination," I said. It sounded to me like another one of her vocabulary-builders.

"The art of foretelling future events," she said.

"Okay," I said. "Foretell me something."

Most of the adults I knew—my teachers, the parents of my friends, the old people I used to deliver papers to—repeated themselves, responded always to what you said or did in predictable ways, moved along in comfortable and reassuring grooves. At some point they'd become human jukeboxes: You pushed a certain button and they sang a certain song. But not my mother. I never knew what she was going to say next. Sometimes she seemed a little crazy to me, sometimes scary, sometimes just embarrassing, but never dull. Now she was going to say something I'd never heard before, and I was glad.

"What do you want to know?" she asked.

"What about the Twins?" I said. "The *Sporting News* picks them for first. What do you foresee?"

She put her cigarette down and let it burn at the edge of the table. She turned over another card—the two of spades—and placed it at the top of a column. She pushed some other cards around then, using her right hand now, her numb one, moving it heavily, as if it were a blunt tool rather than a part of her, a puffy knobbed club. She knocked it against the table a couple of times, awkward but definitive, a flesh-and-bone gavel.

"Doesn't look good," she said. "I don't like what I see. Not one bit."

"What?" I said.

"I see injuries," she said. "An ambulance."

"Go on," I said.

"Somebody being strapped onto a stretcher."

"What else?" I said. "What else do you see?"

"Confusion. Dissension and stupidity. A slow start, an upturn at the all-star break, some sort of streak, and then, in September, a train wreck."

"Sounds familiar," I said.

"I'm sorry," she said. "I call 'em as I see 'em."

I considered asking her some more questions, about me, about us, what was going to happen, how it would all turn out, whether she saw any ambulances in our future, any more police cars for that matter, any dissension in our locker room. But I didn't. She didn't know any more than I did. I knew that. And truth be told, I didn't want to know about any future events. The ghost of Christmas future, its ominous hooded figure, its silent bony finger, even in the Mr. Magoo cartoon, had always terrified me. I didn't want to see whose name was on the gravestone.

"So what am I supposed to do?" my brother said.

"Nothing," I said.

"Talk you out of it?"

"No."

"Shake your hand?"

"No."

"You want me to say that I'm proud of you? Is that it? Give you a nice pat on the head? I'm supposed to admire you or something? Is that what you expect?"

"Nothing," I said. I raised my hands. It was my

father's trademark gesture of surrender exactly. "That's what I expect from you."

"You're really something, aren't you?"

"You said it."

"You're a dumb son of a bitch," he said.

"Sure," I said. "That's exactly what I am. Whatever you say, that's what I am."

"No," he said. "I mean it. I really mean it. You are a dumber son of a bitch than I ever imagined. Beyond my wildest dreams."

When I told Mr. Walker I had something I needed to tell him, he looked apprehensive. I guess anybody would. When someone clears his throat like that, warms up for some announcement, it's like being served with something, signing for a registered letter—how often does it turn out to be good news?

"I'm all ears," he said.

There were some words I had intended to say, and I think I said them. During a unit on public speaking, I'd learned to jot key words and phrases on an index card when making a speech. This day, sitting with Mr. Walker at his kitchen table, my key words and phrases were, I believe, "appreciate," "not right for me," and "sorry."

My mouth was moving, I was making some noise, but I was watching Mr. Walker, trying to gauge his reaction. He nodded his head a little and fiddled with his wedding band, which for the first time, I realized, he still wore, even though it had been almost a year since his wife had died.

I hurried to the end of my little semiprepared statement. Tell 'em what you're gonna tell 'em, our speech teacher used to say, tell 'em, tell 'em what you told 'em. "So," I said. "It's a great school. But it's not for me."

Mr. Walker took off his glasses and cleaned them with a tissue, first one lens, then another, slow and meticulous. Without his glasses, he looked different—flat-eyed, weary and unfocused. But when he put them on, he was himself again.

He asked me if I wanted a Coke. I said yes, and he stood and went about getting one for me, very deliberately—selecting a can from the refrigerator, filling a glass with ice, pouring slowly, handing it to me with a coaster.

"Is it your mother?" he said.

"No," I said.

Mr. Walker might have thought that I was returning another pair of new sneakers at her insistence. That I was underprivileged and was going to stay that way. Which wasn't the case.

I knew you didn't need shiny labs to get an education. Spacious grounds and canoes and a silent auction had nothing to do with it. And the funny thing is I think Mr. Walker must have known it, too. We beat teams in fancy uniforms all the time. Hard work, he used to tell us at practice again and again. Hard work and heart, that's what wins the day.

"I know she's proud," he said.

My mother *was* proud, but the way some people used the word, it meant something else entirely.

"I made up my own mind," I said.

"I see," he said.

He looked puzzled and disappointed. Here I was, a student of the game, doing a stupid thing, making a rookie mistake. Getting picked off with two out in the ninth. I was a broken window refusing to be fixed. My mother was right—he really was Mr. Fixit. But what I could never explain was that somehow I had come to love my broken home, the broken world, all the chipped paint and scars, all that cracked and terrible beauty.

He looked out the window and after a minute said something about spring being in the air. In fact, it was early April, but everything was still brown and frozen.

"Just a couple of days now," he said. "Opening day."

If he had yelled at me, I could've just put my head down, looked hang-dog and waited it out, the old school routine. But that's not how he operated. He was a teacher. He was prepared to work with me, willing to take his time, coach me through it, this little problem I had, this hitch in my swing.

He made his own little speech then, his closing argument—tradition, discipline, fine young men—and for the first time, I think, his patience seemed a little oppressive to me, all that slow, relentless goodness. Part of me wanted to stick a pin it.

In my mind, I had a clear image of a fine young man. He was like a young George Walker, not the real gangly George of the yearbooks, the goofy, grinning Big Train with a handful of baseballs, but some well-scrubbed adolescent version of the middle-aged man. A guy with shiny shoes and a firm handshake. A clean car and a rose garden.

I could have said something smart then, picked up some sharp words and flung them at him. That's what my father would have done. But I knew Mr. Walker was a good man and that I was lucky to know him.

"I want to take your history class," I said.

He looked surprised and pleased, as if he'd somehow forgotten that he taught at the school he'd been trying to talk me out of attending.

"Well, yes," he said. "You should. By all means. Of course you should."

"I'm gonna sign up for your section of driver's ed, too," I said. I wouldn't have to tell him about my time behind the wheel with my mother. He could be the one to teach me about the brake, how to yield, the rules and regulations, all the fine points. From the two of them, my mother and Mr. Walker, I figured, I would learn everything I needed to know.

I raised my glass. I'm not sure why exactly, it just seemed like the thing to do. "Cheers," I said.

Mr. Walker still had the empty Coke can in hand, and he raised that in my direction. "Joy in Mudville," he said.

CHAPTER TWENTY-TWO

I walked home from Mr. Walker's feeling inexplicably light, happy, free. Lucky and relieved. Like school had been canceled on the day of a horrible test. Like a fourth-inning deluge in a game my team was losing. I felt like throwing my hat in the air, like tearing up some important papers. I broke into a run, a measured trot, the way you take the field at the start of a game, confident and controlled. Across the street, Mrs. Gunsher was rolling her wire grocery cart toward the corner store, and I gave her a big wave. I wished her well. This is what it feels like, I thought to myself. *Remission.* It wasn't going to last, I knew, but I figured, so what? Nothing does.

When I stepped into our house, I saw my mother standing barefoot on a chair in the middle of the kitchen, jabbing a fork into the overhead light fixture. She had a couple of screws clenched between her lips and the dusty glass dome in her free hand. She was up on her toes, unsteadily poking around in a tangle of colored wires bunched up behind three dead bulbs.

"For chrissake, Mom," I said. "What are you doing?"

"Home repair," is what I think she said, but with her mouth full of screws, I couldn't be sure.

"You're gonna get fried," I said.

She said something else, which had the rhythm of a wisecrack, but the only words I could make out distinctly were "live wire." Her face was frozen into a ventriloquist's smile, a fixed pained grin.

She pocketed her fork and put her hand on me then, her fingers digging hard into my collarbone, and started the slow process of lowering herself down. When she finally let go of me, she was sitting in the chair, sort of prim but winded, and my shoulder was aching. I could imagine a bruise already forming. My mother had apparently lost the capacity to calculate and control how much muscular force she needed to exert and always seemed to apply too much pressure.

"How about we go for a ride," I said. "Go get something to eat."

"Right now?" she said.

"Sure," I said. "Why not. I'm buying."

I had that chunk of money I'd earned from Mr. Walker squirreled away and this seemed as good a time as any to start spending it.

"What's the occasion?" my mother wanted to know.

"Since when do we need an occasion to eat?" I said.

"Okay, then," she said. "I'm game."

. . .

My brother was slumped on the couch in the living room, dead-eyed, watching a game show.

"Hey, Gerard," I said.

He looked up at me, surly and skeptical, same as always.

"We're going to get something to eat," I said. "You wanna come along?"

He didn't say anything.

"Come on," I said.

I stood there, mute, watching him watching me, not knowing any words that could convince him that this was not a joke or a scam, not a trick or a trap. No concealed weapons. I really wanted him to come along.

When I reached for him, he flinched. I grabbed his arm and pulled him up to his feet, hand over hand, like a tug-of-war with his big inert self. Once he was on his feet, I lowered my shoulder and pushed him toward the door, an indoor drive block, just the way I used to push him across the rink back when I was helping him ice skate.

"What the hell," he said.

I pushed as hard as I could, feeling suddenly that something important was accountably at stake, my arms, I imagined, surging now with some heroic, superhuman adrenaline strength, as if I was trying to save his life, as if he was a drowning man I was trying to pull to shore or a wounded buddy I needed to drag into our waiting chopper. Gerard resisted, but I kept at him— nudged and pushed him out the front door, across the porch, and down the walk, like a big barge headed downriver.

Finally, he had enough. When we got to the curb, he broke out of my grasp and pushed me away. He tugged at his sleeves, straightened his shirt. He looked at me.

"I'm gone," he said.

He spoke it plain and clear, not angry, not as a taunt or an insult, just a statement of fact. He turned then, and I watched him walk slowly away from me.

Without any discussion, my mother headed for the fast-food strip on Robert Street. I must have had almost a hundred bucks crammed in the pocket of my jeans, all crumpled fives and singles I'd earned shoveling Mr. Walker's snow.

"What if we just kept driving?" I said. "How far do you think we'd get?"

"White Bear Lake," my mother said. "If we're lucky."

"Come on," I said. "Think big."

"Minnetonka," my mother said. "With a strong tail-wind."

At the base of the big hill on George Street, stopped at a long red light, I looked out the window and saw something strange in the plate-glass window of a pharmacy—us, our reflection. At first the image didn't register—what I was looking at. The Valiant was smudged with dirt, and I could see rust spots forming on the fenders; something, a broken pipe, some piece of the exhaust, seemed to be hanging dangerously low from the undercarriage. I couldn't see my mother, just her cane, sticking up in the front seat, a shadowy weapon, like the sawed-off shotgun in a cop car. In that window,

I had a kind of mildly demented, all-night, bus station look, squint-eyed and shifty.

We looked nicely disreputable, I imagined.

I tapped my mother on the shoulder and motioned with my thumb. "Get a load of them," I said.

On Robert Street we passed McDonald's and Burger King, all the franchise drive-ins, one after another, our local fast-food Murderers' Row: Dairy Queen, A&W, Clark's Submarines, Kentucky Fried Chicken, Red Barn, White Castle, plus a couple of 24-hour sit-down places, Perkins and Embers. My mother noticed that Heap Big Beef, a new teepee-shaped roast sandwich house that we had been meaning to try, seemed already to have gone out of business—there was a big FOR LEASE sign out front.

My mother drove past them all and turned into the 10 Acres drive-in at the very end of the strip, her personal favorite. Just like at A&W, you ordered through an intercom at 10 Acres and they brought the food to your car. But it wasn't a chain, their hamburgers didn't have cute names, and their root beer was nothing special. What they did have were astonishing crinkle-cut skin-on french fries, cooked in pure lard no doubt, the best in the world as far as we were concerned. My mother, who loved their coney islands, always ordered two with extra onions and a large black coffee.

It was roughly dinnertime, six-thirty, seven o'clock, but there were only two other cars in the lot, a big Plymouth and yellow VW Bug, parked around the side, both of which seemed to be empty.

"Anybody home?" my mother said.

They must have just opened for the season. There was still a pile of evergreen branches piled near a Dumpster, leftovers from the December Christmas tree sale. I could see somebody in a baseball cap moving around inside.

"We're just early is all," I said. "It's opening day."

We always did things the same way: The speaker was on the driver's side, so my mother pressed the red button, and while my brother and I hissed late requests, revisions, and modifications—sour cream on the side, extra ketchup, no ice in my Coke—she, like the spokesman for an unruly delegation at a political convention, placed our order. She always enunciated with a kind of practiced clarity and calm, like a reporter in the field, somehow managing to bring a certain sense of importance, even dignity, to our order.

This time, at the last minute, just as she was wrapping things up, nodding while the tinny voice of the guy inside read back our order, I changed my mind.

"Forget the plain hamburger," I said. "Get me a coney, too."

"You sure?" my mother said, off-mike, and I nodded.

Maybe ten minutes later, a woman wearing a pink nylon parka and a blue ear band brought our food, and while she hooked the tray on our window, my mother half turned toward me and held out her palm. I handed over two of my fives. She paid, exchanged niceties with the woman, and told her to keep my change.

My mother unloaded the tray then, napkins and straws and condiments, peeked inside the waxed paper to see what was what and handed me my things. I undid the door of the glove box, which I used as a tray, and I started tearing open packets of salt. It was a happy ritual, another one of our automotive picnics. As much as the food itself, I loved the activity, passing things around, unwrapping things, how the car filled with the smell of the french fries and the vinegar tang of ketchup.

Before my mother dug in, she wanted to see me eat a coney island.

"I can't believe it," she said. "Mr. Blandmouth is going to eat an onion."

So with her watching me, I took a huge brave bite, crammed my mouth full. It was crunchy, a little sweet, nothing like what I'd imagined.

"Well?" my mother said.

"Fine," I said, still chewing. My eyes were starting to burn a little. "Great," I said. "Out of this world."

After we ate, my mother drove and I fiddled with the radio dial, trying my best to keep Tony Becker's call-in show tuned in, but it kept drifting. I heard snatches swirled in static—a tirade against something or someone, Ali maybe, ticket prices, the commissioner. Like my father's poetry, it was an oddly comforting furious sound, distant rolling thunder.

We ended up somewhere south of the Cities, beyond

Mendota Heights and Rosemount, I believe, cruising down a long unlit stretch of road.

"Where are we, anyway?" I asked.

"Nowhere," my mother said.

"The middle of nowhere," I said.

It was dark now. But it was a clear night, and away from the city lights, the stars were brilliant. It felt like we were in the wilderness. I couldn't identify a single constellation, but I felt the urge anyway, a desire to connect the stars with imaginary lines and make a picture in the sky—a man or a bear, a dog or a dipper, maybe my own pattern, an original.

"You think I'm stupid to turn down an expensive education?" I said.

"I don't know how to tell you this," she said. "But you've gotten an expensive education. The finest."

It seemed funny that I'd always thought of Mr. Walker as the educator, an instructor to the very bones, my teacher and coach.

We pulled up to a four-way stop then, the intersection of a couple of numbered highways.

"Now what?" my mother said. "Where to?"

"Just drive," I said. "Fast."

She put her foot all the way to the floor.

"Hang on," she said.

I watched the red speedometer needle slowly climb: 30, 40, 50, 60, 65, 70. The four-cylinder Plymouth started to shake and rattle then, like a mechanical seizure, and when she hit 75, the ashtray and door locks were vibrating.

I looked at my mother's hands on the wheel. They

were red and puffy, knobby and gnarled as a veteran catcher's, scratched and scarred, fingers stained with tobacco, clamped awkwardly in place. At one time, I was afraid they'd become claws, flippers, monstrous vises. But not anymore. They were human hands, I knew that if I knew anything, utterly human, worn and battered, crippled with disease and punished by hard use, broken down and broken in like an ancient and beloved baseball mitt. I understood—that's what human means. Those hands had caught my fastballs, repaired household appliances with a hairbrush and a fork, deep-fried onions and kneaded dough, pitched melon balls at me, spelled out her righteous indignation on a paper napkin. They'd passed around hot potatoes, flipped off impatient teenagers, tossed firecrackers, cheated at solitaire, signed kited checks, and held a knife at my father. Those hands had grabbed the back-door lock and in a shower of broken glass and blood and murderous curses, held on, held on and on. I knew she couldn't hold on forever. Pretty soon I was going to have to take the wheel.

My mother turned to me and grinned, her foot still pressed hard on what she loved to call the exhilarator. That's how I remember her best, driving our beat-up car, fast, into the night.